GAMER GIRLS
MONSTER VILLAGE

ANDREA TOWERS

Illustrated by Alexis Jauregui

Andrews McMeel
PUBLISHING®

Written by Andrea Towers.
Illustrated by Alexis Jauregui.
Designed by Tiffany Meairs.

Andrews McMeel Publishing
a division of Andrews McMeel Universal
1130 Walnut Street, Kansas City, Missouri 64106

www.andrewsmcmeel.com

23 24 25 26 27 SDB 10 9 8 7 6 5 4 3 2 1

Paperback ISBN: 978-1-5248-7659-3
Hardback ISBN: 978-1-5248-8452-9

LCCN: 2022947625

Made by:
RR Donnelley (Guangdong) Printing Solutions Co., Ltd.
Address and location of manufacturer:
No. 2, Minzhu Road, Daning, Humen Town,
Dongguan City, Guangdong Province, China 523930
1st Printing — 12/12/22

ATTENTION: SCHOOLS AND BUSINESSES
Andrews McMeel books are available at quantity discounts with bulk
purchase for educational, business, or sales promotional use. For
information, please e-mail the Andrews McMeel Publishing Special Sales
Department: sales@amuniversal.com.

CHAPTER ONE

"**C**elia!"

I swivel my head up and notice that my math teacher, Ms. Kenshaw, is staring at me. I guess she has good reason, because she's going over a math problem that I *definitely* didn't solve. What I *have* solved is the shading of the drawing in what should have just been my math workbook.

"Celia?" Ms. Kenshaw tries again. I quickly cover the drawing with my left hand and look back up at the equation. I have no idea what any of it means. Ms. Kenshaw clears her throat. "Can you share your answer for page thirty-eight, problem three?"

Page thirty-eight . . . oh no, I was on workbook page sixteen.

I must look like a deer in headlights, because my friend Jess makes eye contact with me from the seat to my left. Her thumb is pressed into her palm underneath her desk, and I can decipher four fingers jutting out. *Four* fingers. Four? Is that the answer?

"Four," I reply, trying to sound confident. That's one thing my drama class taught me last summer. If you pretend to be confident, people will think you were paying attention all along.

Ms. Kenshaw sighs. I wonder if she *expected* me to mess up, which is kind of rude for a teacher, but she doesn't press. "That's correct. Thank you, Celia," she says, and continues teaching. Next, she picks on this booger-y kid in the back, and I'm safe.

Phew. My hands come together to form a heart back at Jess. I'd love her even if she didn't save my butt, but I especially love her because she did.

I'm sure my other friends would help too; they just aren't in my math class. Up until pretty recently, Jess and I were kind of a trio, alongside our other bestie, Nat. Jess is super smart (clearly) but she's also really athletic. You know how there's always the kid at the back of the group when everyone runs the mile? That's me. And the one at the front? That's Jess.

I guess it would be easy to describe Jess as "the athlete" of our triad, but that's also not her main attribute. Jess is a great friend. She's one of the most reliable people I know for pretty much everything, which I guess is what makes her such a good team player in basketball, volleyball, track, rowing . . . you get the picture. She's also one of the best people to go to the mall with because she'll tell it like it is. An outfit is bad? Jess will say it. Pink or yellow? Jess has an answer. Me? I like to hedge on things. *The outfit isn't bad, it's the length of the skirt. Pink is nice for daytime and yellow for evening.* We could all be a little more Jess in our lives.

Nat, meanwhile, is one of the nicest people I know, even though we joke that she's always off in her own dreamworld. If you think *I* don't pay attention in class, you should really peek at Nat's notebook. It's covered in story ideas and—as I just learned—fanfiction about her gamer-tag alter ego, **Gnat112**.

Nat's a gamer. I didn't know she played video games until two weeks ago, when I learned that she's an *amazing* gamer. I mean, amazing. As much as that girl can get her nose buried in a book, she can also get immersed in a game. She kept the secret for *years*, though, which made me sad at first because who keeps a secret like that from their best friends? Nat wasn't a bank robber or anything. But then Nat told us all about how she got bullied online for being a gamer and I understood immediately. I posted some fan art of my favorite band not too long ago and got **flames** for it. Not the cool emoji flames that mean something is super-hot and cool. Flames as in, people were MAD, all because I made the lead singer shorter than the drummer (the drummer is always in the back, it was his time to shine). Anyway, it's almost like the internet hates everything and can't have nice things, but I didn't let it get to me. Nat, however, *did.*

Jess and I found out that Nat is a gamer because a new girl, Lucy, moved into the house next door and kinda pieced all the clues together. Lucy is *also* a gamer. She just moved to New Jersey from California, and she knows all the hot gossip like who's who in Venice Beach and where most people are getting their jewelry from these days. (I run a papier-mâché earring business, so it's Very Important™ to know these things.) Lucy is great, and she's now the reason we're more of a quartet than a trio.

After Nat's secret identity came out, Lucy and Nat

showed Jess and me how to game. Then we formed our own club called the **Gamer Girls.**

I'm not super into gaming the way that Lucy and Nat are. But I care about supporting my friends. Nat has big dreams of being a streamer, so we started our own Gamer Girls channel to help Nat achieve her goals.

Actually, Gamer Girls is why I was drawing in math class to begin with. See, every cool streamer needs some cool merchandise, and I have big plans for our merch. Like this T-shirt:

And this snapback hat, which is good because **"dad style"** is kind of chic these days.

I'm thinking we need four designs before we go big with merch. Maybe one of those cute stickers for your water bottle and some enamel pins. Or comfy sweatpants to wear to school (even though *I'd* never wear sweatpants to school, I bet Jess would). Or a really cute scrunchie. Or maybe a mousepad, so that other gamers can use it when they game on their computers too?

Gah! So many ideas. I wish Jess could make a gesture underneath her desk and we'd have it all figured out.

Although Jess, Nat, Lucy, and I eat lunch together every day, and hang out a lot on weekdays (when we're done with homework, of course), Friday is Gamer Girls time. And this week, it's our first official stream.

Since I'm not too great at video games, I want to make sure I **bring it** in terms of merch. Highly designed, gorgeous, high-quality merch.

Still, sometimes I wish art had an answer, like problem three on page number thirty-eight. But art is subjective. It lives. It exists. I put my tongue out and erase a bit of the logo. What if that part was purple?

See what I mean?

When I get home from school, Mom and Dad are working, which means they're in their respective offices. Mom fundraises for a big nonprofit healthcare company and Dad is a consultant for a company that builds a lot of big skyscrapers in Manhattan. Although they both work from home, it gets a little lonely when they're stuck in front of their computers all day. (But before you feel bad for me, don't worry. Mom *always* leaves a delicious snack on the counter with a handwritten note. Today, the snack is a guava and cheese empanada, which is my favorite. Her note says, *"Mondays aren't my favorite, but you are!"* Aww. Thanks, Mom.)

When Mom and Dad work, I either create art . . . or, most recently, I game. Nat and Lucy are obsessed with this video game, *Alienlord*, where essentially you blow aliens up. I enjoy watching them play because the graphics are really mesmerizing, but aside from that, there's not much else I like, especially since I don't care for blood or alien guts and my reflexes are probably the worst of all my friends. But that's also why I'm practicing. If I practice *Alienlord* like I practiced playing violin, maybe I'll get a little better. I'd like to last at least five minutes in a game.

I boot up *Alienlord*, ready to get my game on. Nat and Lucy love to play against each other, but I'm still taking on the computer, which means a non-playable program that beginners like me can undertake.

BEEP BEEEP BEEP! My screen goes black. It's been five seconds and I've already lost to a big-headed alien who blasted me a step outside my home base.

"Are you kidding me?" I groan. Then I boot up *Alienlord* again. Five seconds later, I lose another life in the same place. See? I really don't know how this is fun for my friends, but I'm determined to make it work.

I start it up *again.* I make it to a crater this time before accidentally stomping on a poisonous alien plant. **BEEP!** Game over.

I feel like I'm never going to last thirty seconds in this thing, let alone five *minutes.* I stuff half of Mom's empanada in my mouth and crack my fingers, hoping maybe this will release some kind of great gamer juju. After all, fourth time's the charm, right?

This time, I manage to make it past home base, past a crater, and avoid the poisonous plants. *Phew!* I look at my timer. I'm in the game for ten seconds. Then eleven. Then twelve.

I'm doing it! I'm really doing it! Mom's empanadas must be actual magic. She isn't a great baker like Nat's dad is (he owns the best bakery in town), but maybe her recipes give people superstrength in *Alienlord,* and they're filled with guava, so right now, they're my favorite thing ever.

SUPER VIDEO GAME EMPANADA!

At thirty-two seconds, I still haven't been beaten by a good ol' alien pal, but I've also yet to *destroy* any of them, which I know Nat and Lucy would do. (Since that's how you win the game and all.) But winning *Alienlord* isn't exactly my lot in life, and I know this. All I want to do is survive long enough to hang out with my friends!

At forty-two seconds, an ugly orange alien pops up from behind a massive rock. He's too close. There's no way to outrun him. I grab my alien sword like I see Nat do and try to fudge my way with the controllers by spam pressing "B." Wait—no, I meant to spam press "A," apparently "B" makes you jump instead of attack.

The alien is getting closer . . . **Mayday! Mayday!** I strike "A" again when he's close, hoping I did it . . . I close my eyes . . . count to five . . . did I just get my first score in *Alienlord*?

My eyes flutter open and I stare at the screen. Game over. The alien got me.

"GAAH!" I screech. Dad's office is kind of close to my room, so I probably bothered him, but I'm filled with such gamer rage, I can barely contain it.

Nat and Lucy know *Alienlord* like the back of their hands, but I'm such a newbie. And not just to *Alienlord*, but to gaming in general. I feel like a total loser. Ugh.

Then I realize something. *Jess* is a newbie too. There's no way she's faring any better than I am.

I pick up my phone and text Jess. *Are you game for a videocall?* I ask. She shoots back her reply within seconds. *I'm on break at soccer practice. Yeah, give me a buzz when you're ready.*

I hit the "videocall" button on my phone and after two rings, Jess picks up. Her hair is tied up with a pink headband and she looks sweaty—almost like she was defeating aliens herself. Her face looks like a perfectly glazed doughnut, and if I didn't know it was sweat, I'd ask for her skincare routine ASAP.

In my own videocall square, I look frustrated. I try to fix my facial expression, but Jess has already caught me.

"You good?" she asks.

"Yeah," I reply. I fill her in on my *Alienlord* escapades—how I want to make it a few minutes by the Gamer Girls meeting, and how I need to get some designs done.

"No one is expecting you to be great at the game," Jess replies. "Kind of like when I see the Golden Trails Middle School cheerleaders. They're all amazing athletes, and they're so impressive, it's nuts," she smiles. "But I'd make a terrible cheerleader and I know that. Still, we can share the field. Do you know what I'm saying?"

I think about that for a second. I guess I kind of do. Jess has never been a cheerleader, but she's friendly with all of them.

"I think so," I reply. "And you—you're doing okay in *Alienlord*?"

"It's fine, it's fun," says Jess. "It's competitive and

you know I like that. But don't worry, Cece. If you're bad at *Alienlord*, you're not getting kicked out of Gamer Girls or anything. We'll just find something else that you vibe with. Promise."

See what I mean? Jess is an *amazing* friend. And she tells it like it is, very matter-of-fact.

"Okay, thanks, Jess," I say and hang up.

I go back to my designs that I started working on in math class. I know Jess is right—no one expects me to be great at *Alienlord*. But isn't it kind of fake to call myself a "gamer girl" and not game?

CHAPTER TWO

After Mom and Dad are done with work, we eat dinner. It's Chinese takeout today, which is my favorite because it's all delicious—the fried rice, the shrimp—and made even better because we eat out of the cartons, so I don't have to do any dishes.

"How's the gaming going?" Dad asks in between mouthfuls of gyoza.

"It's . . . going," I admit. "I think the game is going better than me, honestly."

Dad furrows his brow a bit. Since he builds skyscrapers in Manhattan, he's all about problem-solving. "What do you mean *busting aliens* isn't artsy Celia's thing?" he teases. "Aren't you an action-packed war hero, ready to suit up and steal the Declaration of Independence?"

"The next James Bond, actually," quips Mom. You know how some people's parents have "Dad jokes?" Well, I've got them from both sides of the family. Mom can hold her own in that regard.

"So hilarious," I reply. "You two should be comedians. Hardy-har."

"Who says I'm not?" asks Mom, wagging a chopstick at me.

I tell them all about how I want to get good at *Alienlord*. Mom and Dad love my friends—okay, maybe not Lucy, since they haven't met her yet—but they know how much supporting my friends means to me, which means supporting Gamer Girls. Mom and Dad had me when they were young, so they "get it" more than some other peoples' parents do, which is nice. And I think a part of Mom *loves* it when people ask if she's my big sister.

"Isn't *Alienlord* an old game, anyway?" Mom asks. She's right. Lucy's dad introduced it to her because he played in college, and Nat's big sister, Dylan, also knows some players. "Why don't you browse the app store and try to find something more your speed?"

Dad hears Mom say "app store" and his eyes bug out. Dad *hates* when I spend money online. He's constantly telling me about saving, and how just adding something to cart isn't a good practice for the future. But he's also not about to say that I can't use the app store.

"Your weekly allowance kicked in yesterday, just don't go overboard," Dad cautions me. (I also think he remembers the time I accidentally bid too much for a rare designer set of booties that didn't fit. In my defense, it *was* in my allowance. Until the express shipping fees from Italy got factored in. Let's just say I didn't get my allowance again for another month in order to pay it back.)

"You got it, Dad," I reply. I scarf down the rest of my shrimp and help my parents put everything away. Even though there's no dishes to do, I rinse the containers and toss them in the recycling bin. I do save a sauce container for Dad, though—he likes to reuse them when he makes his famous tomatillo salsa. Mom likes to joke that Dad is frugal, but if you ask me, I think he's just super smart and not wasteful.

After dinner, I open the app store on my laptop and start looking at some new games. You're allowed to play some demo versions, so I pick a new game that's kind of like *Alienlord*, only more modern. Maybe I'll have better luck against *modern* aliens. The graphics are much better than *Alienlord* (but I'd never tell Lucy and Nat that), and you can customize your avatar completely, including what accent they have. That seems exciting, so I choose a British accent and get going.

The graphics open and I'm a spy in a big city ransacked by alien zombies. *Zombie plotline*, I think to myself. *Very original. Not.* I'm supposed to hit the zombies with my light sword, but it takes me a few seconds before I realize how to activate the light sword at all. And the gaming mechanics aren't very intuitive. Going forward on the keyboard makes me turn backward instead, and the game glitches every few seconds or so.

So I go back to the app store and demo a puzzle game. Only that one's too boring. You're just solving puzzles, '80s style. I feel like my abuelita would love them. I laugh to myself. *Seriously, Celia?* I think. *You're going to be a Goldilocks about* **videogames***???*

I decide to give it one last shot before calling it a night. My mouse hovers over a game on the "newly released" list called *Monster Village.* I kind of hope I don't like this one, because if I go through with the full purchase, it's *all* my weekly allowance, which means I won't have money for anything else this week. The *Monster Village* logo boots up on my computer, and seconds later I'm greeted by a cute monster named Beck.

The monster is so cute, my heart does a happy dance. But also, I'm trying really hard not to like this game, so I fight back the urge to doodle him in my notebook and instead get going.

"Here in Monster Village, you get to design your own town—your own village! For starters, you'll need to decide where to build your home. When you've found the right spot, take the Home Starter Kit out of your ita bag and get going."

Ita bag! They're cute bags with window panels so that you can have enamel pins. I have a few ita bags for the fandoms I really like—mostly, my favorite musicians and their fandom pins. I *love* that this game has ita bags **in the game!** That's certainly something *Alienlord* would never, ever do . . .

"When you're done choosing your home, you'll be able to catch monsters with your butterfly net. The monsters can live in your ita bag, or they can be sent to your home," Beck continues.

I keep happy-dancing. This game is *perfect*. It's adorable and cute and smart and sweet, and I get to *design things*. Sure, it is a bit cozier than the games my friends play, but for the first time ever, it feels like I'm a gamer. About ten minutes later, I call Dad over to tell him that I've found my weekly allowance for the week. Dad clucks his tongue at me, but it's my allowance, so I get to spend it how I like.

From then on, I'm hooked. I customize my furniture, my clothing, the trees around my house. And then, while planting a pear tree, I see a monster so cute that I actually **squeal out loud.** It looks like a pink raccoon-cat hybrid with a really derpy, adorable tongue. I follow Beck's advice—he's the tutorial for the game, I've learned—and guide the monster into my net. *Score!* The raccoon-cat is mine!

I also learn that in *Monster Village,* the bigger your town is and the better it's designed, the more "monsters"—little creatures that look like a hybrid of aliens and animals, or animals and bugs—come out of hiding. It's like constantly having a big multiplayer scoreboard to compete against, even though it's not really a game that you compete in.

After I "catch" the raccoon-cat, who is just as adorable, raccoon-y, and catlike as he sounds, I catch a green hippo with wings that kind of looks like Beck, and a unicorn. I name my raccoon-cat Mapache Gato, since that means "raccoon" and "cat" in Spanish.

I'm so happy. Jess was right—I just needed to find

my *thing*. And *Monster Village*? Well, this is *it*. In between planting some more flowers for my village, I find out there's tons of *Monster Village* players online too. Maybe we can add this to our Gamer Girls livestream on Friday! It'll be a good idea for our channel to expand out of battle games.

I love the game so much, and I can't wait to tell the Gamer Girls about it at school tomorrow. I could probably text them now, but then that would take time away from *Monster Village*—and designing the Gamer Girls merch, which I should probably continue doing.

Huh, I'm starting to sound like Jess, always busy with some sport or another!

CHAPTER THREE

My phone *dings!* in the wee morning, hours before my alarm wakes me up. I open one eye. I was up so late playing *Monster Village,* I even had dreams about it. Mapache Gato was real, and he lived in my room and helped me with some designs.

Half-awake, I reach for my phone and squint at the small text on its too-bright screen.

You up? Important Gamer Girl business!!! reads a text from Nat.

Why are you texting so early? I type back.

Dylan came over to pick up more stuff from storage and woke me up.

Dylan is Nat's older sister. She works for the local animal shelter, and she fosters dogs. She's pretty cool. Dylan used to live with Nat and her family, but she moved out last week and got her own place. It all happened so fast!

Nat was upset when Dylan announced that she was moving out. But Dylan has the coolest new place, or so Nat says (I haven't visited yet). Dylan even has a big gaming room just for Nat—and all of us, once we have the first official Gamer Girls meeting. This works great because Dylan will supervise us too—well, as much as she can. Basically, she'll just make sure that no online trolls get rowdy or too mean and that we're not doing anything that could get us in trouble. And Dad likes that we have someone adult watching out for us, even though Dylan's just graduated from college, so I don't really think of her as an adult.

I know Nat well enough to know if she really wanted to talk, she would keep texting, so I give up and try to go back to sleep. It doesn't work, though, because I'm already up. I pull myself out of bed and resign myself to just being tired all day. Maybe I could pull off a nap or something in math class. Ms. Kenshaw would probably have a fit.

By the time I'm dressed, I'm a little more awake. I'm surprised Nat hasn't texted me again now that she knows I'm up, but I figure she must be getting ready for school herself and she's probably busy. Or maybe she's lost in some early morning *Alienlord* session. Now that I know what it's like to love a game so much, I totally understand! Since Nat and Lucy walk to school together, they're always gaming early in the morning too—even if it's just on their handhelds while they wait for each other to get ready.

I pour myself some cereal and see that Mom has already started the coffee, which means she's been up for a while working. I don't understand how adults like coffee so much, but Mom says maybe I'll develop a taste for it when I'm older.

I still have an hour before school, so I go to my laptop and boot up *Monster Village* again. Each new day, there are some new **"dailies"** for you to complete, like replenish all my supplies, go vegetable shopping (since you can build lures for the monsters with vegetables), and make sure my town is in tip-top shape. (Basically, no tree branches on the ground, no trash anywhere, and no bugs in my house.) This week is apparently also Fishing Week in the game, and the more fish I catch, the more points my village receives. In *Monster Village*, you also get rated every day for your town based on how nice it is and how much stuff you have. I'm set on getting a five-star rating today.

The hour goes by so fast! I hear my dad's voice from outside the door. "Celia! You're going to be late!"

Thankfully, I prepared for school *before* I started gaming. "I'm ready," I announce, grabbing my backpack and heading downstairs. Although I have a few backpacks (it's always nice to change things up), I chose the ita bag today with enamel pins of LTS, my favorite band. *Monster Village* inspired me to wear the ita bag, of course.

Dad gives me a look as he walks to the kitchen and pours some coffee into a travel mug. "I have a late meeting today, so I think we might order out again tonight," he says. "That okay?"

I don't love Dad working late so much, but I *love* ordering out.

"Okay, but I get to pick," I say. "Tacos." Dad makes great tacos (no one uses more adobo than him), but El Cocinero across the street comes close.

"Anything for you, **mi querida**," says Dad.

"Mi querida" is Spanish for my darling, which my dad likes to call me. We don't really speak Spanish at home, because Dad hasn't spoken it since moving away from Mexico when he was a kid. And Mom doesn't really speak it at all since she didn't grow up with the language, even though she's Cuban. But my dad started calling me mi querida when I was little and when we would have our "special time" together playing or reading books. Sometimes I wish I was better at speaking Spanish.

Dad drives me to school. When I get out of the car, I see Nat, Lucy, and Jess already congregated together in our usual spot.

"Miss Celia has *finally* arrived!" Nat exclaims, handing me a chocolate–cherry mini muffin from her stash. Nat always brings extra pastries from her dad's bakery every morning. It's kind of a tradition.

At this point, I ate breakfast two hours ago and I'm a little hungry, so I shove the muffin into my mouth. It's so good that I immediately resist the urge to grab another from the container that Nat is holding.

"Okay, well now that we're all here, I have some *news*," Nat says.

Jess, Lucy, and I trade smiles. I want to be annoyed that we all woke up so early for Nat's text, but I know we're all on the same page of just wanting to be happy that our friend is excited about something.

"Sorry to keep you guys in suspense. I just had to confirm one last thing," Nat says. (I love Nat, but I'm a little dubious of this—more than likely, Nat got lost in her own little world.) "Look!" Nat holds her phone out for all of us to see.

"It's a **gaming competition!**" Nat says. "MegaBox *just* announced it late last night. And in a few minutes, they're going to reveal which game is going to be featured for the contest."

"No way!" I exclaim.

I see Lucy cast a glance at me, like, *really?* I guess

that makes sense. I'm not one to share the excitement for this kind of stuff. MegaBox Studioz is the gaming studio behind *Alienlord*, but it's also at the helm of *Monster Village*, or so I learned last night.

Meanwhile, Nat smiles right at me. I know she was worried for the longest time that I wouldn't be into gaming, so I'm hoping the genuine excitement makes her feel more at ease. (Apparently, she thought that because I made fun of some old arcade games at a pizza shop one time. But what Nat *didn't* know is that I just thought the arcade games were germy. I mean, who's cleaning those, anyway? I just saw pizza grease hand after pizza grease hand on them. I'd rather spend pizza tokens on pizza than grimy ol' games.)

"The contest is *mega cool*," Lucy smirks, proud of her joke. "And it's a good thing they're announcing what game it will be soon. We still have time before the first bell rings."

With two minutes to spare (and three minutes until the first bell—sometimes I wonder if my middle school *specifically* makes the bell ring at 8:01 in case kids—or, more likely, teachers—are wrapped up in things like this), Lucy pulls up MegaBox Studioz's livestream. We all huddle around her phone.

My brain is buzzing with MegaBox Studioz's announcement. *Alienlord* is an old game, but it's popular with a niche crowd like Nat and Lucy, so that could be what the announcement is for. The studio has had some other hit games too, mostly other battling and competitive ones. I'm sure that whatever it is, Nat will be the first to try her skills.

All I know is that it won't be for *Monster Village*, because there's not much you can broadcast as fun and competitive in the game, especially since the town ratings are pretty quiet. That's also the point of *Monster Village*: to have fun in the art space and make friends with cute creatures like Beck and Mapache Gato. I smile, thinking of Mapache Gato and the veggies I'll collect for my afternoon dailies when I'm home.

"Look, it's starting!" Lucy squeals.

There's a woman gamer named TimberTina21 announcing the livestream, and I sneak a glance at Nat, because I know that's her ultimate dream: to be a successful streamer with her own channel. That's kind of why we started Gamer Girls—we wanted to do it for our friend group, of course, to have a place to play and show people that girls could game just as well as anybody else. But we also wanted to help Nat with her dreams. And what better way to do that than have your friends support you?

Nat looks excited, her eyes scrunched up and her pupils moving back and forth quickly. I know she's probably focused on the announcement. I bet she's hoping it will be for *Alienlord*.

Jess and I peer in closer as Lucy groans.

"Oh my gosh, just announce it already!" Lucy says in exasperation, looking up quickly and glancing at the school doors. "We gotta be in class in *one minute!*"

"Shh, it looks like they're showing something," Jess says, gesturing toward the phone.

We all watch together as a huge logo comes up on screen. It starts as some colors first, first purple, then pink, then blue . . . then some lighthearted music . . . a set of wings . . . a hippo's face . . .

My hands feel cold. I'm in a state of numbness, which I guess is shock? The last time I felt this was . . . never.

"*Monster Village*," Nat says, reading off the screen.

I stare as Nat, Lucy, and Jess trade shrugs.

"Never heard of it," Lucy says.

Never heard of it! I want to scream. *This is my game! My thing! I was waiting to show my friends how to play anyway!*

BRIIING! The first bell rings, but we're all still gathered by Lucy's phone. We have one full minute to walk to class anyway, so I steady my breath and focus on the announcer's voice.

"And there you have it, folks—MegaBox Studioz's big announcement this morning is for the latest game in their portfolio, *Monster Village.* In this lighthearted game, players create a village inhabited by monsters that you also get to catch. If you haven't played it, get ready, this one's a goodie." The livestream slide changes and now it's about details for the contest. "In conjunction with MegaBox Studioz, I'm pleased to announce the contest is to design a whole new town that will be featured in their promotional ads. The winner of the contest will get to see their town in ads all over the country. They'll also get to demo the latest DLC before anyone else, and for free."

I can barely contain myself. Like I said, downloading *Monster Village* was my whole allowance for the week, so getting their DLC—an update to the game—for free? Well, that would be *epic*.

"I wish *Alienlord* were coming out with a DLC," Nat remarks.

"Yeah," Lucy adds. I haven't said two words yet, but I can tell they're a little disappointed. "Does anyone play *Monster Village?*"

Finally, it's my time to shine.

"I started it last night!" I yelp, probably too excited for my own good. "And I *love* it." My brain is buzzing. *Monster Village* was so unlikely to be the studios' announcement, and I started playing it mere hours ago . . . it feels like this is fate. Like I was meant to help the Gamer Girls with this.

Now, Nat flashes a smile at me. I can see the excitement trickle back onto her face.

"No way, Celia! That's amazing. You'll have to teach us!" she says. "And we'll need to figure out what designs to submit. We can talk about it at the next Gamer Girls meeting on Friday."

I nod eagerly. I'm about to share more intel on the game—like that it's Fishing Week, or that the music is just the best—but the second (and final) bell rings. The last thing I need right now is detention, so we book it.

I just know I'm barely going to get through history when there's *Monster Village* to think about.

CHAPTER FOUR

At lunch, Jess has already scored a table for the four of us, which is good because in middle school, finding an open lunch table is pretty much as impossible as finding a lost earring in the ocean. (I've made that mistake before.)

I don't have a handheld console like Nat and Lucy do—I game only on my laptop, or with one of them—so Nat takes out her own console and downloads the free demo for *Monster Village*.

"If we win this contest, it will take Gamer Girls to the *next level*," Nat says, beaming. "We'd be on the map—literally, since it's about a map of the neighborhood, but also worldwide, since our name will be on the promos."

I can feel my cheeks get red—something Mom always chides me for. But I can't help it. I can imagine it now—Cece79, winning for Gamer Girls. I wouldn't be a fake gamer, I'd have every right to be a Gamer Girl, and Gamer Girls would be internationally known! Nat would have a platform for her streaming channel, we'd have bragging rights . . . I'd have the DLC . . . I can think of nothing better.

I show my friends how to make their avatar and start designing their villages. "And you can collect cute monsters in your ita bags, just like the one I've got here," I say, showing off my ita bag.

I help Nat catch a monster (a cute white and black dog with a red beret named Farfel) and make a few stops around town, visiting the grocery shop and picking out new vegetables. Then I open the customization tool so I can design some new walkways for Nat.

As I'm sharing all of this with the group, I can see that Nat and Lucy are a little impatient. Lucy is practically squirming. Nat is less enthused than she was ten minutes ago.

"So," Lucy says, eyeing the game. "What's next? Do you . . . **battle the monsters**?"

"Nope," I reply. "You collect them!"

"There's no minigames? No two-player arena?" Nat asks.

"No, none of that," I say. "Well, you can visit someone else's village, so tonight you can visit my village, Nat, but there's no battling. It's about building something—creating it. It's really fun, I promise."

"It's like, the opposite of *Alienlord*," adds Jess.

Nat and Lucy exchange glances.

I'm feeling defensive all of a sudden, which is odd, because I've never felt like this with my friends before. "You have to give it time," I say. "I think you're going to really like it once other things open up. Like once you find a fishing rod, you'll be able to participate in Fishing Week and catch some aquatic monsters."

"Oh! Is *that* a minigame?" Nat asks.

"No, it's fishing," I reply. "You fish and catch more monsters. But it's great. And they can live in your house, or you can add a fish tank attachment to your ita bag in the game."

"Hmm," says Nat.

"I'll make sure to invite you to my village tonight," I reply. "Then you'll see how fun this game really is." I make Nat add me—**Cece79**—as a friend.

Everyone has a special name they use in gaming. It's called a gamer tag. Nat's is Gnat112 and Lucy is

Spyder_0wns. Me? I'm **Cece79**. I chose the name because Cece is what my parents have called me since I was a baby, or my best friends, and the numbers are because of my birthday: July 9th. I know that Nat thinks of Gnat112 as her own kind of alter ego, and that's also how I think of Cece79. Cece79 is what I wish I could be. Someone who is wholly devoted to her art. No math or history to intervene.

When I arrive home, Dad left out some duros de harina, which are these crispy little fried wheels that are delicious with some hot sauce and lime. I scarf down a few, finish my homework (which isn't much—it's kind of a light week at school), and text Nat. I really want her to come to my village so that she can see how cool the game is. Plus, I need to start brainstorming new and unique maps for the contest.

Before I can finish composing the text, however, I hear a soft *ping!* from my phone. Jess has group-texted the Gamer Girls a new photo of the karate belt she just earned. As I start to type back some congratulations (although to be honest, I didn't realize Jess *also* does karate now, in addition to her zillion other sports), Nat sends a new text.

Yaaaay Jess!!! Also, any chance you're free right now? I know it's not an official Gamer Girls meeting, but I'm helping Dylan with her foster dog and I'm a little overwhelmed . . . maybe you can help me?

A few more texts roll in, and the impromptu friend hangout seems solid. I run downstairs to Dad's office (Mom's door is closed). His late meeting hasn't started yet, so I get there just in time. "Can I go to Dylan's place?" I ask. "Homework's already done. Jess's mom will pick me up and drive me back. *And* there will be dinner, so it's a raincheck on tacos." Since I answered basically all his questions, Dad agrees. Besides, his late meeting is happening, so he kind of can't say no.

While I wait for Jess and her mom to pick me up— my house is on the way to Dylan's from the karate studio—I pack my laptop. I don't take it to school, but it can come with me to Dylan's.

My laptop is kind of old. It was Mom's old work laptop, and she gave it to me when she upgraded her own. But it works just as well, and Mom doesn't even mind that I have a budding sticker collection on it, mostly of LTS. I make a mental note to find a cute *Monster Village* sticker online when my allowance sets in again so that I can have more fandoms accurately represented. Hooray!

About thirty minutes later, Jess texts me that she's outside. I wave at her mom as I get in the car and buckle my seatbelt.

"Congrats again!" I say to Jess, who is beaming over her new belt. "Mrs. Johnson, you're going to need a whole room devoted to Jess's trophies soon."

Jess's mom laughs.

"I'm sure your mom says the same thing about your art."

It's true—Mom does. When I was little, she'd put my drawings on the fridge, like basically every other parent out there. But then I kept making art, and we don't have the biggest house, so it expanded to the bathroom walls, Mom and Dad's offices, and finally, a glass case by the kitchen for my arts and crafts.

If you ask me, I think my parents love that I'm into art. They both have very left-brain minds, so it must be exciting to have a kooky, artsy daughter.

Mrs. Johnson's car arrives at Dylan's apartment and Jess and I tumble out. I haven't seen Dylan's new place yet, so when I get out, I realize it's nice. Most recently, she fostered a Beagle named Max, but he just got adopted by a nice elderly couple with a big backyard, which Nat says is good for him since he likes to sunbathe. I know Nat was kind of bummed because she loved Max, but it was in his best interest, and that's the whole point, after all.

I've always thought of Dylan as a few years older than us, but she's twenty-two, which is a whole nine years. Of course, I've known that Dylan is an adult for a while, but she didn't really feel like an "adulty-adult" until I see the official-looking mailbox out front that says, "D. Schwartz."

Lucy arrives not even a minute later, and Nat meets us outside. "Come on in," she says. "Dylan's on a walk right now, so we have the whole place to ourselves for a second."

Inside Dylan's apartment, I glance around. There's multicolored party lights in the bathroom, tons of hanging plants, and a stack of board games so big, it makes my head spin. (I didn't even know there were that many different board games in the whole world!)

"Well, this is where the magic happens," Nat says, leading us into her lair. It's small—about the size of a tiny attic—but it's a nook that's just for her, with a gaming chair and three poufs for the rest of us on the floor. I make a mental note that the walls seem kinda bare. I think some art could really spruce them up.

"Welcome . . . to the **Gamer Girls' Den!**"

Jess "oohs" and "aahs," and Lucy does too. Lucy's a fast talker, so she's immediately rattling off a ton of new ideas for the room. "Oh, it's great that it's set up for really fast Wi-Fi—and we should probably soundproof the room so we don't bother the other tenants in the building—and maybe have a jar of dog treats in case one of Dylan's animals bothers us during a game—and we can set the stream up here—"

Speaking of Dylan's animals, I hear a *click* at the door and a sniffing nose. A bunch of feet scatter and run into the Gamer Girls' Den.

"Whoa, whoa!" I yell as I trip backward, landing on my butt with a hard *thud*. Dylan's dog of the moment is really large, and he's *definitely* letting me know that he's in charge.

MOVE JOYSTICK TO DODGE!

"Francis!" Dylan yells back as the dog takes off and runs out of the Den, back into the open living room. "Ugh, sorry, Celia . . . Francis, come here!"

I pick myself up off the floor while Dylan grabs the dog. She's so commanding, the dog obeys pretty much immediately. Lucy looks at me worriedly as I brush myself off and get up.

"You okay?" she asks.

"I'm fine," I answer, because I really am. "Just got a little surprised and fell."

"Sorry," Nat apologizes. "I met him the other day and he was good."

Dylan comes back from wrestling with the dog.

She's also very apologetic, but I reiterate that it's okay. I've never had a pet aside from a goldfish when I was in second grade, so the jumping was just new to me. I feel a little silly.

"Francis is calm now, if you want to pet him," Dylan tells me. I do as instructed and hold my hand out first so that he can smell it. Dylan says this is a good gesture because it shows Francis that I'm not a threat. Once he's sniffed it enough, I pat him on the head. He's very fluffy and reminds me of a monster, if *Monster Village* characters were real!

"I'm heading out to see a movie with some friends, but in case there's an emergency, my phone's on vibrate, so call twice and I'll come ASAP," Dylan tells us. "And there's some money for pizza on the counter as a thanks. Just make sure to clean up after yourselves—I don't want any ants."

"You got it," says Jess.

"Roger that," Lucy says.

"Bingo," adds Nat.

I nod.

I check my bag quickly to make sure that nothing has fallen out or gotten broken—namely, my laptop. Everything looks okay though, so I put my bag on one of Dylan's tall bookshelves and out of Francis's reach. Dylan wishes us all good luck and heads out.

With Dylan gone, Nat drags a big bag of dog food from her pantry into the kitchen and scoops out three cups for Francis to eat. (Big dogs need a lot of food, I guess!) Francis starts chomping right away, which makes me smile because he has a knack for getting the kibble everywhere.

"I brought my laptop so you can come visit my village," I announce to everyone. "And I'd love to show you all what I've done with the place!"

"Oh," says Nat.

Oh? That's . . . not the reaction I was expecting. I started gaming *because of Nat*, after all, so this less-than-enthused response seems . . . out of character for her?

"Is everything alright?" I prompt.

"Look, Celia, I *love* that you love *Monster Village*, and I think that's awesome, but I was also thinking about it, and maybe *Monster Village* is just not for me," she says. "I don't think I'm going to get the paid version. Or participate in the contest. I'm sorry."

Lucy's bites her lip. "Me too," she says. "I played after school today. I really tried to get into it, but I kept wanting to, like, blow something up."

I'm a little stunned at their response. They were so excited about the MegaBox contest earlier, and now they're just dropping it altogether?

"Why?" I ask, in a voice smaller than I meant to.

"I just—well, *Monster Village* isn't really a game I'm good at," Nat admits.

"You only played it for about twenty minutes during lunch," I point out.

"I know, but it's . . . **different**," Nat argues.

"Different how?"

I can see Nat getting visibly uncomfortable.

"I'm used to being *good* at things!" Nat says. "Like *Alienlord!*"

"You're the *best* at *Alienlord*," I agree. I make eye contact with Lucy. "You both are. But that doesn't mean you can't be good at *Monster Village* too."

"Maybe," Nat muses. "But if I don't get to be *great*, I don't know if I want to try. That's silly, isn't it? But it's how I feel."

"That makes sense," adds Jess. "It's like I told Celia yesterday. Some people are great cheerleaders, and some people are great track runners. Maybe *Monster Village* just isn't your thing, Nat."

I bite my lip. I don't want to start an argument with my friends, but I'm disappointed. After all, I supported Nat when she revealed her gamer secret, even if Jess was upset that Nat never told her. I don't think it's intentional, but Nat is basically quashing my *Monster Village* dreams like she was afraid I'd do for her *Alienlord* ones.

"Well, maybe we can still game together," I suggest. "If you still want to visit my village—"

"I just think we should do something that we *all* like to do," Nat cuts me off.

Now I feel even more annoyed. It's not like I love playing *Alienlord*. It's not really my thing the same way it is for Lucy and Nat. But I try it, and I do it, because we all help each other out. That was supposed to be the point of Gamer Girls . . . right?

I think Nat can sense that I'm kind of sad because she shakes her head at me. There's real sorrow in her eyes. "Look, Celia, we'll talk more about it at the official meeting on Friday," she says. "I *promise*. I have some new streaming ideas for us to try too, so we can get our numbers up."

She turns and walks away, motioning for Lucy to follow. I walk behind my friends slowly, trying not to show my disappointment and attempting to convince myself that I'm overreacting about my feelings. I'm still going to enter the competition and design the best village for the promos, but it would be nice if I got some support from my BFFs.

CHAPTER FIVE

I leave Dylan's place tired and sweaty. Wrangling Francis took a lot of work! When I get back to my own house, however, I'm surprised to find my abuelita sitting at the table, drinking tea. Her long silver hair falls around her face, held up with a clip in the shape of a butterfly.

I'm one of the rare people who is close with their abuelita—at least, it seems that way. I spent all of last spring break with her. But still, it's unusual to have her visiting during the week.

"Abuelita!" I say as I run into the kitchen. "Why are you here? Is something wrong?"

Abuelita laughs. "Nothing's wrong," she answers. "I promise. I had a doctor's appointment in the city and your mom said I should stop by before going home."

"Oh." I guess that makes sense. I drop my bag on the floor, careful not to jostle my laptop too much.

"How's school?"

"Good," I answer, because there's not really much else to say. "Just a lot of homework. My friends and I are doing a video game thing."

"Friends? Any boys?"

I know it's usual for adults to tease kids about potential crushes, but I've also never told her what team I play for, so I don't like that she assumes. Dylan likes everyone, for example. Me? I haven't really decided yet—crushes just aren't my thing. "Abuelita!" I cringe, shaking my head. "*No!*"

Okay, I guess that's not *entirely* true.

See, there is *one* boy. But I don't really like him in *that* way, because I'm not looking for any kind of boy to be *with*. I just like him because he's supportive of Gamer Girls. His name is Liam Porter and he goes to our school. Whenever he sees Nat or Lucy with their consoles at lunch, he says something nice, like how great they are at *Alienlord*. He doesn't interact much with us outside of that, but when someone's supportive of my friends, they're supportive of me, and what can I say? I dig it.

Nat was kind of into him earlier in the year and

Lucy likes to call him a **"well-rounded hottie"** because, in addition to liking gaming, he plays drums for the school band and, apparently, he's in all the honors classes. I don't know if I agree with the "hottie" part, but he does have some cute floppy hair. I wonder if Abuelita can tell I'm lost in my thoughts, because she prompts again.

"Everything else okay?" she asks.

"Yes," I answer, sitting down in the chair across from her. Abuelita raises an eyebrow.

"What's wrong?"

"How do you know something's wrong?" I ask.

Abuelita gives me a look.

"Okay, it's not that *nothing's* wrong," I amend, leaning forward with my elbows on the table and eyeing the plate of candies that have been left out. "I'm just a little annoyed."

"About what? Did something happen in school?"

I bite down on my lower lip, debating whether to share. It would take a lot of explaining if I really wanted to tell her everything.

I take a deep breath. I guess if I don't tell her now, she'll continue staying in the dark, and that's not nice.

"Okay, so I found out there's a contest happening for this game I really like, *Monster Village*," I explain, swinging my legs back and forth under the table. "I was super excited and wanted to do it with my friends because it's a game I think we can all get behind. But my friends aren't interested. Nat said that she didn't want to partake in the contest because she didn't feel like she was good at *Monster Village*. I said we could do it together, and she said we should do something we're *all* good at. But that's not fair! I mean, I should get to do what I want even if my friends don't like it, right?" I finish the sentence all in one breath; it feels like I've just run a marathon.

"Hmmm." Abuelita nods along with my story. When it's done, she hands me a candy from the bowl next to her. "I wonder if your friends are **jealous**."

"*Jealous*? Of what?" I take the candy from her hand, unwrap it, and shove it into my mouth. My friends can't be *jealous* of me. I'm not even good at gaming compared to them!

"Maybe they're jealous of you being good at something they're not good at. Celia, I hope you are right and it's not that. And hopefully you can work things out, so you're not upset," she answers. "But I'd remind you to have some empathy for your friends. It's not fair to you, but it's not fair to them either. Now. Can I have some tea?"

"Sure," I say, a little snippy, although I'm glad to have a reason to change the conversation. "One tea coming right up."

I get up and walk to the counter, making Abuelita a cup of tea. (I know she hates that it's not the "traditional" way, like from a kettle, but she knows I'm not really allowed to use the stove too much so it's okay.) After bringing it to the table, I grab my bag.

"I'm gonna head upstairs for a little bit," I say.

"Okay, Cece. I'll be here." Abuelita smiles and waves as I walk out of the room.

Once I'm upstairs in my own bedroom, I pull out my laptop from my bag.

Was Abuelita right? Were my friends *jealous* of me? I mull over the idea in my head, but it just makes no sense. I can't see how my friends would be jealous over a game they don't even care about playing much.

No, I tell myself, feeling confident in my thoughts. Abuelita is fantastic, but she doesn't know what's really going on. She just knows the basics of the whole situation; she didn't see the sorrow in Nat's eyes as she admitted she didn't want to play *Monster Village,* and it would be impossible trying to explain that. Adults are hard like that sometimes—they always try to tell you what they think because they had a lot of different experiences growing up. I know Abuelita probably had her own friend issues to deal with at some point. But she doesn't know *my* friends, not the way we are now, and she's never even met Lucy. The only kind of real fight we've had was when we found out Nat didn't tell us she was a gamer. And even then, we weren't really mad. We were just perplexed, Jess more than me, and we worked it out quickly once we understood why she'd kept her secret.

This is totally **different.**

CHAPTER SIX

The next few days are pretty monotonous. School, *Monster Village*, friends. Nat and Lucy are back to playing *Alienlord*. Nat asks me how *Monster Village* is going from time to time, but I can see the interest she had at first has waned completely. And Jess is playing Switzerland, meaning she's not getting involved. "Call me when you're playing a sports game," Jess said when I tried to approach the subject. Like I mentioned earlier, Jess tells it how it is, and she is just uninterested in getting involved. I respect that.

I do think Nat and Lucy feel kind of guilty that they aren't into *Monster Village*. On Thursday, Lucy asks me if I want one-on-one tutoring in *Alienlord*, so that I can play alongside her and Nat. But I explain that *Alienlord* isn't interesting to me. It's just blowing aliens up. And *Monster Village* is . . . well, it's **magical!**

"You're both saying the same thing, you know," says Jess. "Nat and Lucy don't want to play *Monster Village*. You don't want to play *Alienlord*."

"And you don't care for either of them," I remind her sharply.

"I care for my friends," says Jess.

By Friday, I've started building my new village for the *Monster Village* contest. The submissions have to be in by Sunday the fifteenth, which is . . . sixteen days away! I've also continued work on the Gamer Girls merch; I'm hoping I can debut them at the same time. Maybe if I win the contest and simultaneously create the merch, Nat and Lucy will be forced to admit *Monster Village* is a viable game that's good for the channel (bringing us more views and merch orders!).

When I get to Dylan's apartment for our first official Gamer Girls meeting, Lucy, Jess, and Nat are already settled into the living room and eating chips from a big bowl. Dylan lets me in with a smile. The one lock of her hair that she always dyes is fuchsia today, and she has big, crystallized skull earrings hanging from her ears. Skulls aren't my vibe for jewelry, but on Dylan, they look gorgeous.

"Cece! Now that you're here, it's time to commence the first-ever Gamer Girls meeting and livestream!" Nat announces.

"Technically second," adds Jess. It's true—we did all game together before, the day we found out that Nat games. Nat busted out some alien butt-kicking moves that had all our jaws on the floor.

But that's neither here nor there.

"So, I was thinking, for our first order of business, we'd talk about the gaming we did this week, then any housekeeping, and then get to streaming," says Nat. "That way it's fair for everyone. And we get to talk about all kinds of games."

I smile. *See?* I want to tell Abuelita. *My friends* do *care about different games! It was all in my head.*

Everyone agrees that this is a good agenda for the first—and all—Gamer Girls meetings.

Lucy starts us off and prattles on about how many wins she's had in *Alienlord*. Apparently, she and Nat have been battling it out a *lot* while Jess and I were busy. Lucy is the newest member of our friend group, but I'm glad that she fits right in. Jess and I were nervous at first—what would the new girl be like?—but she's super awesome and has a lot of the same interests as Nat, who we used to joke was kind of an oddball. Though to be honest, the four of us are kind of oddballs. We aren't uncool by any means, but we also aren't the popular kids at school, like Mel White, who is super nice and has her own makeup channel.

Nat then regales us with how many times *she's* beaten Lucy. If you ask me, it seems like they've beaten each other an even amount, but I smile because they're so ultra competitive, they'll never agree just how many.

"Take a tally next week," says Jess. "And dessert's on the loser. Mostly because I want dessert. Volleyball practice today made me **huuuuuungry**."

Next, Jess talks about her own gaming. She hasn't had much time since her schedule's so packed, but she's played a few games of *Alienlord* against the computer, and she started building her own village in *Monster Village* with the demo.

I kind of want to ask her which one she prefers, but I don't.

"Celia?" Nat asks, prompting me to speak up next.

"Lots of *Monster Village*," I reply. "I figured that

I'd try out for the contest. I know you guys aren't into it, but if I win . . ."

"That'd be **epic**," says Nat, and I beam. See? They are supportive! It was all in my head!

Next, we discuss housekeeping, which is general order of business. We knew this already, but Nat reminds us out loud about her agreement with Dylan. We aren't allowed to stream on our lonesome, mostly for safety reasons, and since Dylan's an adult she'll supervise us when we're on the camera. I think Dylan is there mostly to protect us from trolls. As a "thank you," we must make sure we don't leave a mess anywhere. When we're not streaming, we're still allowed over, but we have to tell Dylan's landlord, who lives in the building. I guess this happened the other day when Dylan went to see the movie.

Jess is up next. She can't attend next week's meeting because she has a track meet. "Unless we move it to earlier in the week?" She suggests. We're all free on Thursday, so next Thursday it is.

Then it's my turn. I've been waiting for this. I open my laptop and pull up the designs I've created for Gamer Girls merch. I share the T-shirt, the snapback hat, a scrunchie, and a pair of sweats *I'd* never wear, but Jess would.

"I think the merch will appeal to a lot of gamers who are also girls," I say. "And I want to take away any bad associations people have with gamer girls. So the design isn't too try-hard and it's unapologetically awesome female energy. We'll start wearing it at first to promote us as a brand, and then we'll sell the merch online or at local comic cons, if we make it there."

The Gamer Girls logo is designed with pixels to mimic old-school games, and I've also added a slogan on the back of the hat that says:

"Oh my gosh," whispers Lucy. "This merch. Is. Perfect!!!" Her eyes light up.

"Eek!" I squeal. "Do you really like it?"

"Like it? I love it," adds Nat. "How fast do you think we can get it? Maybe we start sporting them on our livestreams, and direct people to an online store?"

"We can probably get prototypes fast," I reply. Like I said before, Mom works in fundraising, so she knows all about making merch quick. "And maybe put up a Kickstarter or something for the rest of it? With Dylan's permission, of course."

"Heck yes," says Nat.

My cheeks turn red again. I've been nervous about the merchandise collection. I make my own jewelry, and Mom helps me sell it online and at the occasional local craft fair, but this is my first-ever branded line, and I wanted to make sure it looks good.

Suddenly, I feel like a million bucks.

Jess remembers she has something else too.

"It'll be quick, I promise. I know we want to start gaming," she says. "But I was chatting about Gamer Girls with the other kids at my karate studio, and I was wondering . . ." she looks a little nervous. Oh no. "We're not, like, an exclusive group, right? Like if we wanted to game with someone who's not a girl, that'd be allowed, right?"

Huh. I hadn't thought about that. On the one hand, I love that the four of us have created a little quartet. On the other hand, having an exclusive group isn't very nice.

We take it to a vote. Thankfully, it's unanimous.

"That's also another point of Gamer Girls. To inspire more girl gamers. Well, not just girl gamers. **Underrepresented gamers**. But we're the Friday night squad," Nat says. "So, basically, we're definitely open to other people, but if we cast a wide net, Dyl's place will be flooded, and I'm not sure we can throw a big gamer rager. In fact, I'm sure we can't. But we'll cross that bridge when we get there. Maybe the four of us stream, and we support gamers everywhere?"

We all nod. It's a plan!

Now that housekeeping is over, it's time to . . . start the stream!

Dylan walks over and helps us queue up the webcam. I film it, since I'm used to filming things at drama camp.

"What are we playing?" I ask. I'm feeling pretty good, and like Jess said, sometimes friendship is about finding ways to compromise, so I say, *"Alienlord?"*

Nat and Lucy exchange a look.

"Well, I thought we could stream us playing *Monster Village*," Lucy answers. "It's the biggest thing right now since everyone is talking about the contest. So, maybe we should hop on the trend while it's popular and see if we can get some good streaming numbers? Celia, do you want to start us off?"

"Yes!" I proclaim excitedly, pumping my fist into the air. This feels *great*.

We all grab our headsets from a pile in a basket. Nat and Lucy have their personal headsets, being long-time gamers and all, but Jess and I use some of their old pairs. To make it my own, I add some flower stickers to the sides of them. Jess keeps hers as-is, which are royal blue.

"I looked at a tutorial online," Jess admits. "There's a lot of sporty stuff I can make for monsters. I can pretend they're the US women's soccer team."

Lucy finishes setting up her ring light and playing with the settings. Then she moves so she's next to me,

Jess, and Nat. "Ready for the intro?" she asks. We nod. We decided that we should have a standard intro for our stream every week, so that people know who we are. And since we're trying to get people to tune in to our stream weekly, we like to be consistent. It's basically **brand management 101.**

"I'll do the introduction," Lucy says. "And then we'll pass it to Celia, since she probably has the most well-prepared town out of all of us. That'll get people interested, since we'll look like we're *super* good at this game. And then we can take turns showing off our own towns. Cool?"

"Cool," we all echo.

Dylan watches as the camera pans on us. Then Lucy clears her throat and waves happily at the camera.

"Welcome to the Gamer Girls channel! My name is Lucy, and I'm a proud gamer girl. It's Friday, which means we'll be doing some streaming for you. And today we're going to be playing everyone's favorite new obsession—*Monster Village!*" Lucy throws up her hands and we all cheer enthusiastically.

"Now," Lucy continues, "I know *Monster Village* isn't a battle royale game like you saw last time when we played *Alienlord*, but it'll still be fun. I promise. Today we're going to take you on a tour of our villages and show you some cool designs, houses, and more. You might even get a sneak peek at the village one of us is entering for MegaBox Studioz's contest. I hope you can all join us for what's going to be an *epic* Friday night of playing!"

Nat gives me my cue to move into position and take over. I project the game onto Dylan's big screen computer so that everyone can see.

"Okay, hi everyone! Welcome to the official Gamer Girls stream!" I take a moment to glance at the chat log and notice a few familiar names from last time signing on, so I decide to call them out. "Hi. YeleWithAYe! Hi, Rosie580!" I wave enthusiastically. "It's so good to see you back again! Today, as Spyder_0wns said, we're playing *Monster Village*! Some of you might know me from last time, but I wasn't doing much of the gaming, so if you don't, no biggie. I'm Cece79. I'm here today to welcome you to **Cece's Creek**—that's my village's name, if you didn't know! Today, I'm going to show you what I've designed for my village so far and talk about some of the monsters I've collected. And I'll even tell you a little bit about how I made all the stuff I'm going to show off."

I've been putting on a show ever since I was little, so doing it on a stream feels natural, even if it's not a subject I *wholly* know. I mean, if you told me three weeks ago that I'd be playing with a game I spent my whole weekly allowance on, I wouldn't believe you. But here I am, totally loving it.

I enter my village, which is super pristine and perfect (I made sure to pick all the weeds before arriving at Dylan's place). Then I get lost in the world, walking my character around the fictional place I know so well, jumping over bridges and puddles and opening doors and climbing a taqueria I've constructed.

I show off all the special things I've created—storefronts, special walkways, and castles built out of seashells. I'm only vaguely aware of Nat, Lucy, and Jess offering commentary behind me, but their words don't even register because I'm so intensely focused on what I'm showing off.

". . . and that concludes our tour of Cece's Creek!" I finish, smiling at the camera. "If you loved what you saw, stay on for more Gamer Girls tours of *Monster Village*, coming soon after this quick break!"

I smile to myself as I switch off the stream and grab a drink of seltzer. I've been so engrossed in my own head, I haven't even realized the chat on the side of the screen has been going nuts. When I'm done drinking the seltzer, I see that comments are still popping up, even as I take off my headset.

Gouda_Rockz: OMG that was the best stream EVER!!!

FiveThirtyTenGO: Cece79 is soooo good at this game! I need all her designs! Monster Village *rules!*

Kat2008: Okay, where can I go to get the Cece Creek design stuff?? Is it downloadable?

I turn around to find my friends are looking at me

with wide eyes.

"Whoa, Celia," Nat says, super impressed. "That was . . . *sublime*."

Nat once read a thesaurus for fun. I smile.

"Really? Thanks!" I reply. "I mean, I was just enjoying myself."

"Yeah, but I didn't know you made all that stuff!" Jess adds. "I mean, I knew you were designing things, but that was incredible."

I peer around at my friends and my smile grows bigger. It's nice to feel like I'm good at something that I'm not really known for.

"Who's next?" I ask, looking around the room. Lucy and Nat exchange glances, and both of them reach for their consoles.

"I guess I can go," Lucy says.

She puts on her personal headset, and I get up so she can take her place on the gaming pouf. She plugs in her own console, allowing her own village to boot up. The first thing I notice is that it doesn't have as many buildings as mine does. It looks like she's put maybe five or six minutes into the whole game, and I see she's still in the demo version. But I try not to fixate on that. Plus, I didn't even know she made a village at all. She's trying to get involved for me, and that's **+10 XP for friendship**.

Lucy turns the ring light back on and presses the button to load the channel, straightening her shoulders. She smiles at the monitor, showing off all the confidence she usually carries with her when she's gaming.

"Hi, streamers! Welcome back to the Gamer Girls channel! I hope you all enjoyed our first *Monster Village* stream. Now, we're going to look at my own village—**Spyder's Sanctuary!**"

Lucy moves her joystick and presses a few buttons on the controller, starting her tour. As she does so, I look at the chat space. I try not to notice how a few people who had tuned in during my tour are dropping off while she's going through her village. It's not a huge number, but there definitely isn't as much chatter as there was when I was doing my town tour.

As Lucy moves around, I notice there are large swatches of land that are just blank, because she hasn't bothered to build anything or put anything there. And she basically has no monsters in her town except for a few that I know come at the very beginning when you start before you actively start collecting more.

Lucy's tour is over pretty quickly. There isn't much to show, after all. But I know I should be supportive. Again, it means a lot that she tried.

"I can't wait to visit Spyder's Sanctuary with Cece79," I announce when Lucy finishes showing off her town, switching the channel off again.

Lucy looks up as she takes her headphones off. "Really? I'm not so great at this." She makes a face. "I thought people stopped commenting because they weren't interested in what I was showing them."

"Viewers always taper off during a stream," I lie, because I don't want her to know she's right. "Or maybe they were just a little quieter because they were *watching*. After all, where does Spyder_0wns spend her *Alienlord* downtime? A super cool sanctuary."

"That's nice of you to say," Lucy replies, looking at the computer as if she's trying to double-check what I'm promising. "I just know I get a lot of comments when I stream *Alienlord*. Like, I'm *always* talking with other people."

"Well, every game is different, right?" I ask. "I mean, that's what you told me and Jess when we started learning how to game."

"Yeah," Lucy says. "But I dunno . . ."

"I'm not too great at *Monster Village* either," Jess says. "And, I mean, none of us can bake Nat's dad's cupcakes. And I'd like to see *you* guys try to clear a hurdle. In the rain. After face-planting on the ground."

"I'd stay on the ground," Lucy says mock-solemnly.

We're all laughing now. I glance at Nat. She looks content, but I wonder what she's really thinking. Am I stealing her moment?

"Hey, it's your turn," I say to Nat. "Why don't you show off your village?"

I watch Nat's eyes carefully. They flicker for a second, but I can't tell what she's thinking. "Maybe next week," she replies. Nat has anxiety, and I know that even though she wants to be a big gamer, sometimes it's hard for her to be in the spotlight. So I don't argue. But I wish this was something we could do together.

"Jess?" I ask.

Jess shakes her head.

"I think the people want to see you, Celia," Jess says calmly.

Shrugging, I pull up my work-in-progress design

for the *Monster Village* contest. My theme for the contest is basically a whole village that's shaped like Mapache Gato. Home base is on Mapache Gato's nose, and each stripe on his back is a strip of forest.

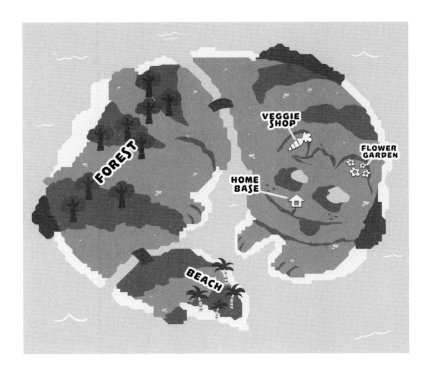

After I show it off, our hour of streaming is done, so Nat ends it.

"Thank you all for coming to our stream tonight!" she says. "Have a great rest of your Friday, and we'll catch you next *Thursday*. **One for all, and all for Gamer Girls!** Good night!"

We power off the stream. Lucy packs her ring light away. Then Dylan squares her eyes on me, from just outside the Gamer Girls' Den.

"You're something special, you know that, Celia?" she says. "I gotta keep you in mind when we're repainting the shelter."

CHAPTER SEVEN

When I get to school on Monday morning, the first thing that happens is Nat shares her dad's leftover apple crumble bites. The second thing? I walk toward my locker to grab a few books. And the third? I hear my name being called.

"Ceeeeeeeeelia!"

I turn around, confused. Whoever is calling out for me is doing so in a singsongy way. I've just broken away from Nat, Lucy, and Jess, who are headed to their own classes because apparently none of us are allowed to have class *or* homeroom at the same time. (It's not something that's intentional, but we still complain about the scheduling.)

The owner of the singsongy voice is Mel White. Her perfect blonde hair trails behind her like a veil, and she's probably the tallest middle school student, well, to ever grace a middle school hallway. I give my best smile and wave. Mel White is perfectly nice, and she used to be Nat's neighbor, but we aren't exactly friends. What does she want from me?

"Uh, hi," I say.

Not too long ago, Mel White started her own makeup channel and garnered a ton of engagement, followers, and important sponsorships. Mel White still regularly "humble brags" about how popular her channel is, especially if she gets attention from big-name celebrities or brands. I used to think she was being ridiculous, but now that the Gamer Girls are in the streaming business too, I understand why she does that a bit more. Sometimes you must talk big to play big, and Mel White knows how to **play big**.

Still, I'm surprised to see she's coming up to me. Other than being streamers, we don't have anything else in common.

Mel White's always been super nice—almost *too* nice. It's one of the annoying things about her. You want to be frustrated that things come so easily to her and she gets so much attention, but she's always nice to everyone, and if you complain about her, it sounds like: "Mel White invited me to her birthday party. Ugh."

She stops a little bit in front of me.

"Ceeeeeelia, how was your weekend?" she asks, dragging out the pronunciation of my name like no one I've ever heard before.

"Um, it was good," I answer, opening my locker. "How was yours?"

"It was nice. My mom surprised me with a visit to Bella's Tea House, and we had their cranberry scones," Mel White replies with a big smile. "Have you tried them yet?"

Bella's Tea House is an old school English–style restaurant. It's also one of the most popular places in our county, thanks to all its old-timey décor where it's designed to look like you're in England in the 1900s. But it's impossible to eat there because they're so busy. They book reservations, like, months in advance, so unless you know someone who knows someone, you're out of luck. I've been trying to get Mom to call so we can go for my birthday in the summer, but so far, she hasn't had any luck finding a spot. *Of course* Mel White would just go there, so very casually, on a random Sunday. It's very **Mel White** of her.

"Anyway, I wanted to chat because I heard you're

really good at that game, *Monster Collection*."

"Um—*Monster Village*," I correct, although I can't believe what I'm hearing. Mel White doesn't really strike me as someone who games—in fact, when Nat and Lucy went to her birthday party not too long ago, she made it clear she didn't. Maybe some of her gamer friends had watched our stream and said something to her? I didn't see their names pop up on the screen, but since everyone goes by a secret gamer tag, it's possible.

"How did you know I play?" I ask.

"Oh!" Mel White looks surprised. "I overheard Liam Porter talking about how he saw you on that Gamer Girls channel. He said you were good, and he has excellent taste, so I always believe him."

"Wait, Liam talked to you? About *me*?" I ask. It's my turn to sound surprised. Liam always has a kind thing to say about Nat and Lucy, which is the reason I think he's nice, but he's never said anything about *me*. Or so I thought.

"Well, Liam didn't say that *to* me," Mel White corrects. "I just heard him talking to his buddies. But he said you can play really well, and I love spotlighting other women, so I was wondering if you wanted to come to my house and play the game?"

"Come to your house . . . **and game**?" This conversation is getting weirder and weirder!

"Yeah. Like, maybe you could guest-star on my channel. I know it's usually about makeup, but I think we can find a way to weave it all in. And of course you can plug the Gamer Girls stream."

I stare at Mel White, a little unsure of how to answer. I guess I'm staring too long, because she pipes up again.

"Oh—of course you'll want compensation. I always ask for a little something when I partner on other people's channels too," she says, very professionally. "One of the companies Mom works for sent me some samples of the *Monster Village*–inspired makeup that's out soon. I'll give you one of each set. Ah! That's perfect—I can demo the makeup and you can game. See? So awesome! And it would be great to collab—two gals from the same middle school! I think it's a win-win for both of us getting to show off how *good* we both are at what we do. Don't you agree?"

"Um," I blurt.

I go over my thoughts in my head. I honestly don't know what to say! It should feel easy to say yes. Like Mel White said, being on her channel *would* be great exposure for Gamer Girls. But I also know I'll have to explain this to my friends. The point of Gamer Girls is to do it *together.* I can't exactly go on the show without my friends, right?

"Well, I usually stream with Nat, Lucy, and Jess," I say. "Could they come on too?"

She doesn't drop a beat.

"I was thinking for this episode, it would be nice to spotlight *you*," she replies. "I love Nat Schwartz, we go *wayyyy* back. And Lucy is so sweet. And our school trophies would be nothing without Jess. But this is one time where I think you should star. You know? You're the best *Monster Village* player at this school."

See? She even manages to say "no" in the politest way ever. It's like she's mastered the art of saying "no" but making it so that you don't even think she did.

I don't love to admit this, but Mel White's words are kind of nice. *The best* Monster Village *player at this school.*

If that's true, that means I really do belong in the

gaming world. And that I might stand a chance in the contest. And that I have my thing—my own special place. That's all incentive enough, but I know I must clear it with my friends—and my parents—first.

"Well, I hope you think about it," Mel White says, as the bell starts to ring. "I think it could be fun. But no pressure. Just let me know. See you later!"

She waves and turns, walking down the hall. As I mosey over to class, I feel like I'm going in slow motion, my brain trying to process the conversation.

There's a lot to digest. But also? There's a tiny, *tiny* voice inside my head that's **super** thrilled Liam Porter was talking about me.

CHAPTER EIGHT

By the time lunch rolls around, I'm still thinking about my conversation with Mel White. I'm lost in my own world, which is usually Nat's modus operandi, so I know I can't hide that something's on my mind when I see my friends. But I'm not sure I've processed it fully yet, so I've gotta come up with something else.

"What's up?" Lucy asks as soon as she sees me.

"Nothing," I answer quickly. "Just, uh . . . some people came up to me and told me they heard about our stream on Friday, and that they really liked my *Monster Village* tour." It's not a total lie, at least. Mel White counts as "some people."

"Oh, cool," Lucy says.

"Maybe we should play more next time," I say as I dig into my peanut butter and banana sandwich. "The game was number one on the app store's most downloaded list yesterday."

Jess, ever the mediator, chimes in.

"I don't know," she says. "I think we can play something different for our next livestream. Maybe we should rotate, and one person picks the game each week. Week one was Nat, week two we played *Monster Village* with Celia, maybe week three is Lucy's choice? And then it'll be my turn."

It's a good idea, but *Lucy* picked the game last stream, not me.

Don't let it get to you, says a voice in my head. *Besides, you really need to focus on the contest this month. And maybe this Mel White situation. The last thing you need on your brain is trouble and drama with your best friends.*

"I guess it makes sense," I admit, taking another bite of my sandwich.

The conversation keeps going. Nat and Lucy launch into a discussion about some huge match they had this weekend while they were playing *Alienlord*. Jess reminds them about the tally they agreed to take. Lucy finally admits that Nat broke a big record and now she's one of the **top scorers** in the game out of a bunch of people who play regularly.

I listen to it all intently. I remind myself that Nat was supportive of me, and it's time to be supportive right back.

Surely, they wouldn't mind if I guest-starred on a Mel White livestream, right? Especially if we're not even streaming Monster Village *as the Gamer Girls this week?*

The rest of the afternoon is uneventful, although I am a bit laser-focused on Liam Porter's hair during science class. At the end of the day, when I pick up stuff from my locker, Jess appears with her hair up and her gym bag slung over her shoulder.

"Celia, I know you better than probably anyone," she says, and it's true. I've always felt a little closer to Jess than anyone else, mostly because we've known each other the longest, even by only a few months. "I could tell something was up at lunch, and if you don't feel comfortable telling Nat and Lucy, that's your **prerogative,** but I really hope you feel comfortable sharing with me."

Prerogative was our English word of the day. It's an oldie, but Britney Spears is iconic, so up until now, my only association was with her song. According to

Ms. Sutker, "prerogative" means "a right," as in, a person's right to do something.

I haven't answered for a beat, so Jess gives me *that look*, the one that says, "the jig is up," and I know I must confess.

"Okay. Well, Mel . . . White asked me if I wanted to collaborate with her. Like, guest-star on her channel and play *Monster Village*," I admit.

If Jess is mad, she doesn't show it.

"Does Mel White even play *Monster Village*?" Jess asks.

"No," I confirm. "I think she just wants to use me as someone who plays because she heard I was good. But she has some makeup products she got based on the game and wants to do, like, a team-up thingy together. I'll also get free makeup out of it."

Although I've never been a makeup aficionado, I think most of that is because makeup is expensive, and it's never been part of my allowance. I usually save that for fashion, paint supplies, LTS merch, stuffed animals . . . okay, basically everything cute but makeup.

Jess doesn't respond right away, and I know she's silent because she's thinking about how to answer. Also, maybe because she knows I'm not going to like her answer.

"Well, are you going to do it?" Jess asks.

"I don't know," I admit slowly. "I've been thinking about it all day. Nat and Lucy would probably be mad, right? They want to be streamers, not me."

"I don't know how they'd respond," Jess says. "But I think if they're mad about anything, it would be you *not* telling them. Remember how angry I was when we found out Nat was keeping her gaming a secret from us? Remember how mad *you* were?"

"I wasn't mad," I purse my lips together in frustration because I sort of feel like I need to defend myself. It's not like I'm trying to cause trouble with our friends! I know I must come out with it; I just need the right time.

"Mel White—well, she *does* have a lot of followers. Maybe it could be a good thing. I mean, I was thinking I could use my time on her channel to promote Gamer Girls and get more people to watch us. Mel has such a big channel, you know?"

Jess nods. "Yeah, I know. But do *you* want to? That's my question. Feelings aside, is your answer yes, or no, Celia?"

"I still have time to decide," I say. "But do you think it would be a bad thing?"

"Well," says Jess as she follows me, a slightly sour look shadowing her face, "I'm not sure it would be a *good* thing, if that's what you're asking. But we're all best friends. I'm sure it'll all shake out."

Jess Johnson. She tells it like it is.

CHAPTER NINE

The next day, I finish perfecting the sketches for my T-shirt and snapback hat. I'm still working on the rest, but we can get going with these designs now. I hand over all my work to Mom, who promises me she'll be in touch with the manufacturer about prototypes.

"Just make sure there's four," I say, so the four of us can have merch. "Then we'll place an order at a later date and sell the rest to our fans."

Mom chuckles. "You got it, Celia," she says.

I decide to tell my friends about Mel White's offer on Thursday, at the next Gamer Girls meeting. Because it seems like official enough business, I could probably sneak it into our housekeeping section of the meeting. Plus, bringing it up at Dylan's over a bowl of chips seems a lot more palatable than hashing it out at school.

For the next two days, I try to keep a clear head. I know there's a ton of stuff I can focus on to take my mind off things—my homework, my friends, the MegaBox Studioz gaming contest—but not much helps. I end up playing a lot of *Monster Village*. The game relaxes me—maybe it's the calm music, or the fact I get to create, or the adorable monster-animal hybrids, but it helps my wandering mind settle.

Jess knows my secret, of course, and occasionally at lunch, she looks into my eyes and says, "Anything you want to share, Celia?"

I make puppy-dog eyes back. "Just a lot of *Monster Village*," I reply, which *also* isn't a lie.

Lather, rinse, repeat.

Thursday after school, I hear my mom's voice filter up the stairs. "Celia! Say hi to Abuelita before you leave!" she hollers. Abuelita's here? I race down to the kitchen but see she's on the phone with Abuelita. I take the device from her outstretched hand.

"Hola, Abuelita," I say.

"Cece! How are you?"

"I'm okay."

"Are you sure?"

"Yeah." I pause, checking to make sure my mom has left the room. (She has.) It's not that I don't trust

Mom, it's that I don't need her snooping around. "I have to tell my friends something and I'm worried it'll make them mad."

"Is this about the video game from earlier?" Abuelita asks.

"Sort of . . ." I trail off and tell Abuelita all about Mel White and her channel. "I mean, it's not about the video game so much as it's about me being good at it and gaining some fame. But I know when I talk to my friends, it'll make them mad. Ugh. We formed the Gamer Girls to game together, not be on someone else's channel alone."

"It sounds like the Gamer Girls was formed to support one other, not make each other feel terrible," Abuelita counters.

I love my friends and I know we *do* support each other. But as smart and wise as Abuelita is, she just didn't deal with this kind of stuff when she was in eighth grade.

"I'm just nervous about telling them," I admit.

"Nervous about telling them? Or nervous about doing it *yourself*?" Abuelita asks.

I let her question hang above me in silence. Is *that*

what I'm so worked up about? Gaming without my best friends with me?

Not too long ago, I'd never gamed before. So, I guess, to some degree, having my friends by my side has been a safety net. I mean, if anyone called Nat a fake gamer, she'd probably throw a **freezing potion** at them. But me? Well, they wouldn't be entirely wrong. I kind of *am* a fake gamer. I only started gaming for real last week, and it's not even one of those big, impressive games.

Abuelita takes my silence as thought. That's a nice thing about Abuelita—she knows not every statement requires a response. "Well, good luck, mi amor," she says. "Let me know how it goes and I'll see you soon."

"You got it, Abuelita," I say.

My mom walks back into the room so perfectly timed, I wonder if she's been listening to the conversation. But she says nothing as she takes the phone back and finishes the conversation, nor does she say anything as I climb into her car and we drive to Dylan's place.

When we arrive at Dylan's, Mom hands me a bag of yuca chips to share with my friends.

"Have fun, and let me know when you're done," she says, and she gives me a kiss on the cheek.

"I will," I promise. Although what I'm promising is the second half of what she said. I can't promise I'll have fun, but I *can* promise I'll let her know when I'm done. So it's technically not lying.

"Oh, and Celia? One more thing."

"What is it?" I ask.

"The manufacturer called me while you were at school today. She says the hat and T-shirt will be available tomorrow."

"*Tomorrow?*" I squeak. I've made things before, like earrings and jewelry, but this is my first time working with a *manufacturer.* And my things are ready. Tomorrow! I can't wait to tell my friends. This also sweetens the whole Mel White thing. If I wear the T-shirt and hat to promote Gamer Girls on Mel's channel, I'm still an agent for all of us, not just me! It's perfect. Maybe all my problems will be solved, thanks to Mom's impressive work.

Mom scoops me up into a hug. "We'll pick it up tomorrow after school. Until then, have a great time with the Gamer Girls!"

"Thanks, Mom," I say. I can hardly believe it. Hello, runway!

I grab my bag—carefully packed with my laptop, just in case we do end up playing some *Monster Village*—and exit the car, scrambling into Dylan's house. The door is already open, so I walk up the stairs where I can hear Nat, Lucy, and Jess talking loudly. Just like last time, I'm the final person to arrive.

"Celia!" Lucy exclaims when I enter. She sounds excited and her headphones are already sitting on her head. "Okay, let's hurry up and get housekeeping over with, so we can move on to the good stuff—streaming."

"One thing from me today," says Nat. "Francis is meeting a potential adopter right now, but he'll be back later tonight. So don't be surprised when a **big dog** comes running in." She smirks at me, and I know she's making a joke.

"No agenda items from me," chimes Jess.

"Celia?" Lucy asks.

Two seconds into the meeting, and I already must come out with it. I take a second to put my bag down. Is this *really* the best time?

I see Jess meet my look. Jess knows, and I can't chicken out now.

"Well . . ." I start. "Okay, so I know this is kind of weird, but Mel White asked if I'm interested in playing *Monster Village* with her. On her channel. Like, together," I finish, getting the words out in a rush.

There's silence. I look at Jess first, who smiles a little bit; she's pleased that I took her advice about telling everyone the truth. I meet Lucy's gaze; she seems like she's processing what I just said. Nat, meanwhile, has a funny expression. I can't tell what she's thinking.

"Uh," I say. "Is that—is it okay? If I do that?"

More silence. *Uh-oh. I'm done for.*

Then Lucy breaks in.

"Okay? Of course it's *okay*, Celia!" Lucy says. "I guess I just want to know . . . why? At her party, Mel wasn't interested in my console at all. What makes her so into *Monster Village*?"

I explain that *Monster Village* is coming out with a line of makeup. I leave out the Liam Porter part of it. Because let's face it, the Liam Porter stuff is totally not relevant at all, and I haven't thought about him since Mel White mentioned it—definitely *not*.

Nat's staring at me as if her eyes are going to pop out of her head. She squints, like she's trying to look for something she can't see. "I think it's a **cool idea**," she says at last. "But is there any way . . . we could all be on it? Maybe?"

My heart sinks.

"Mel White specifically said she just wants me on the channel for right now," I reply, "but I think that if I do a great job, I can talk a lot about Gamer Girls, and our stream, and it'll help us all out."

Nat is quiet for a moment. Then I can see the confirmation on her face. It *is* a good idea. Mel White's makeup channel does have some celebrities who frequent it, and while they may not be gamers, all publicity is good publicity, right?

Speaking of publicity! That reminds me!

"Oh my gosh, and I totally forgot to mention it because it only just happened! The prototypes for the first Gamer Girls merch will be in tomorrow, and I'll debut it on Mel White's channel. Wearing the hat and T-shirt will *definitely* bring us some fame."

Now everyone's excited.

"Whoa!" says Lucy. "That's **baller.**"

"It's a great promotion opportunity," Nat adds.

I beam. Jess and Abuelita were right—I'm *so* glad I learned from Nat's mistake and came out with the secret. I feel a lot lighter than I did only a few minutes ago. The Gamer Girls *are* a super supportive bunch, no matter what!

I don't feel *completely* at ease, though, because this means I still must play *Monster Village* on Mel White's channel, which is . . . harrowing.

Now that all our housekeeping—or should I say, *my* housekeeping—is out of the way, I sit back as Lucy readies her headset again, turning on the ring light and preparing for a new stream. Dylan pokes her head out from the kitchen; it smells like she just made some tomato soup and grilled cheese. I glance at Jess, who gives me a quick thumbs-up. Kind of like in Ms. Kenshaw's math class, we get each other. We're communicating without speaking.

I give a quick thumbs-up back. Jess is right—it did all work out, almost too perfectly.

CHAPTER TEN

Dylan's dog walker, Christine, brings Francis back not too long later, so we pause the stream. Christine says the meet-and-greet went well, they're just waiting on references and vet records to see if he's a good fit. Apparently, potential dog adopters need a *lot* of requirements. That makes me kind of happy, though, because I know Max is with his best forever family, and soon Francis will be too.

Francis bounds into the room excitedly but stops when Dylan shouts out a command that makes him halt in the middle of the room.

"I wish *I* could get him to do that," Nat huffs, as Francis lays down like a happy little lapdog.

Dylan laughs. Today, her dyed lock of hair is bright blue. It swings back and forth in front of her face as she moves her head.

Even though I have tons of cousins, my parents,

and Abuelita, sometimes I wish that I had a big sis like Dylan. Maybe they'd give me some more contemporary advice—or wouldn't work all the time so we could hang out a bit more.

"Fostering a dog is hard," Nat says.

"Not as hard as gaming," Dylan answers, sitting down on the floor with us. "And don't say it's not true."

I've always liked Dylan. People would probably think that someone who graduated college wouldn't be interested in hanging around with middle schoolers, but Dylan's just always been that nice and that cool. When I say Dylan's nice, I'm not talking about Mel White nice, where she's overly sweet just for the heck of it. Dylan's genuinely been nice to us for almost the entire time we've known Nat. And she's been Nat's best friend, aside from us, since forever. I guess it comes with the territory of growing up with a sister who's a lot younger than you, but I appreciate it.

"So, what's today's scoop?" Dylan asks, bumping shoulders with Nat as Francis puts his head in her lap. "Any **trolls** I need to take care of?"

Luckily, we haven't gotten many trolls since we started Gamer Girls, because I think people realized that not only are we *good* at gaming, but we are also fun to watch.

"Just one user during a Spyder-Gnat match on headset yesterday who tried to tell us we picked the wrong weapon in this new gaming style," Lucy says, rolling her eyes. Although not official Gamer Girls streams, Lucy and Nat sometimes game together on the channel. (And they *still* haven't determined who has won more games, so dessert's on no one this week.) "He made a whole big deal about it in the comments and tried to explain it in a way that he knew would make himself sound good. But he just looked silly."

Nat giggles. "He's a mansplainer."

"Annoying, but relatively harmless," Dylan says with a nod. Then she turns to Nat. "I might be going out with Marc on Sunday. Can you help with Francis while I'm gone? I think it'll be a good time for you to bond. He's really learned a lot recently and you can practice some of his new commands with him."

Marc is Dylan's partner. According to Nat, Marc is nonbinary, so we use the "they" and "them" pronouns for Marc. Things are getting a little serious between them according to Nat, but Dylan still hasn't introduced Marc to her parents.

"Sure," Nat looks around at us. "Would anyone want to help?"

Dylan laughs. "Of course," she says, looking around at us. "You're all welcome here with Francis so long as you promise to take care of him and not wreck my apartment *too* much."

"Aw, I was thinking of bringing my baseball bat to swing around inside," chides Jess.

"Hardy har," replies Dylan.

Quips aside, now that we're *finally* ready, we boot up the stream. Lucy does her patented "Gamer Girls" intro for people who are just tuning in, and we position ourselves behind the camera, waving and smiling.

I'm taking a backseat today because it's *Alienlord* day. So, I cheer on my friends and watch as Lucy and Nat get into a big battle. Jess ends up joining them in a three-player match, and although she doesn't last as long as they do, she does get one alien.

"She shoots—and she *scores*!" Jess calls out.

I imagine her dunking the alien in a basketball hoop and smile.

Things are going to be just fine . . . right?

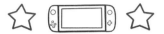

When I get home, I unpack my laptop, turn it on, and start *Monster Village.*

I know I just came from Dylan's and spent most of the night gaming with my friends, but none of it was *Monster Village.* And, well . . . I kinda missed playing it. I wouldn't say it's become an addiction or anything, but it helps calm me down or it takes my mind off of things. It's like when I create art, except it's a different kind of art. I know Mom and Dad do the same kind of thing when they watch telenovelas or read books after a long day of work.

My phone **pings!** just as I'm working on making an intricate triangle design on a rug I've put together in *Monster Village.* I look over and see that it's a message from Mel White.

Hey, Celia! Did you decide if you could play on my channel?

I put my game down and pick up my phone. The decision's been made and I'm feeling okay about it. I also kind of wonder if Liam Porter will be watching the stream. I don't know if he watches Mel White's makeup channel or anything, but it's nice to think about him watching me play *Monster Village*.

Yeah, I'm going to do it. Thanks for the invite!

Cool! Wanna come over on Sunday?

Uh-oh. We had all *just* agreed to help Nat watch Francis on Sunday.

I'm busy on Sunday . . . Saturday OK?

I don't bother to mention the plan, Nat, or Gamer Girls. I'm not sure if Mel White knows much about our whole stream, and I'm not trying to sound ungrateful. After all, she is offering me a nice opportunity. I also realize that although I've known her for years, we've never hung out one-on-one. We usually vibed together at school, or at Nat's dad's block party, or at a Schwartz family dinner since Mel White lived next door.

There's a long pause, then three little dots appear, showing Mel White is typing a response.

Okay, fine. We can do Saturday. See you at noon!!

I put down my phone, staring at the messages.

Well, I think. *That's it. I can't back out now.*

I pick up my game again and play a bit more, at least finishing the design of the rug. Then I hear a knock at my door. "Celia?"

I reluctantly put down my game and look up. "Come in," I say. Now that I'm in eighth grade, my parents respect my boundaries enough to knock whenever my door is closed. They used to just barge in without any warning. Once I got upset about them walking in on a big painting I was making for their anniversary, and they sat down with me, we talked, and they got better about it.

Dad walks in and smiles at me. "How was hanging out with your friends?"

"Good," I answer. "We had fun!"

"Great," Dad says. "I know it's late, but I wanted to make sure I talked to you before you went to sleep for the night."

I feel my hands go cold. Dad is never a big, serious talker. What's going on?

"Is everything okay?" I ask, my mind cycling through all the possible things that Dad could be asking about. Abuelita, my mom, school . . .

"Nothing's wrong," Dad assures me, as if reading my mind. "But I found out that I'm going to have to spend a lot of time *in* the office to prepare for a presentation, so Mom is going to be taking you to school next week. Okay?"

I know "in the office" means in his actual company's office, not his home one. Dad started working at home a few years back and it's nice, but I know his boss likes face time every so often too.

"Oh." I smile at my dad. "Yeah, okay. Sure."

"I know we haven't been around lately, but—"

"Dad, you and Mom are **workaholics**," I point out, interrupting him. I'm not trying to be mean about it, it's just the situation. My parents do support me— like driving me places or making sure to have dinner together—but it's also the truth. Dad sighs.

"I know. Hopefully once this big project is done, we'll be able to spend some more time together. Maybe you can even show me that video game you like."

"Really?" I look at him with interest, since I didn't know Dad was interested in video games at all. "You wanna learn how to play *Monster Village*?"

"It reminds me of some video games I played when I was your age," Dad replies with a grin. "Maybe *I* can show you a thing or two."

"We'll see," I laugh.

Dad's feet pitter-patter away, and I switch my

Monster Village setting from Cece's Creek to the village I'm building for the contest. Today, I add a new row of rosebushes on one of Mapache Gato's stripes. It looks like some awesome shading, and I feel proud of it. I just hope MegaBox Studioz—and Mel White's followers—like it too.

CHAPTER ELEVEN

At school the next day, Nat doles out her dad's new creation, cake jars—literally, cake in a jar—and they're so delicious, I finish mine in one minute.

"Well, I hope the rest of the day goes as sweet as this!" I exclaim. "Then we're in for a real treat."

And in fact, it is a good day. In math class, Ms. Kenshaw doesn't call on me even once, and during lunch, Nat shows me a new feature in *Alienlord* that I kind of like. You can now customize the hit points and attack bar of the aliens. Lucy's dad packed her some malatang that smells amazing, and Jess says she's being considered for the higher-level team in volleyball.

As for me, I cannot wait until after school, when Mom promised that the Gamer Girls merch would be done. I practically sing when the bus drops me off and I burst into the house, ready to go.

But when I arrive at home, I see that Mom's office

door is closed, and she hasn't left a snack on the counter for me either.

At five o'clock, Mom still hasn't opened her door. I'm done with all my work, so I head upstairs and start plucking some weeds that sprouted during the day in **Cece's Creek**. I manage to catch another hippo with wings and do a little dance because it's an elusive shiny one. Then a half hour passes. Then another . . .

It's six o'clock now, which is pretty much dinner time, and I *neeeeeeed* to see the Gamer Girls merch.

I knock on Mom's office door. "Mom?" I ask. "Are you done now?"

Knocking on my parents' doors during the workday is pretty much a no-no, but I figured that since it's late, it's a Friday, and Mom promised we'd go, it should all be okay. A few moments later, Mom shuffles out. She's wearing a mishmash of sweatpants on bottom and business on top; this isn't unusual, though, nobody ever sees the lower half of her body anyway. But I do see that her eyes look extra crusty today.

"Cece, is everything okay?" Mom asks.

"I'm just checking on the Gamer Girls merch," I reply. "You said we'd go after school, remember?"

Mom's face falls. Which is saying something, because she didn't look exactly perky earlier.

"I'm so sorry, Cece, I got wrapped up in the fundraiser—do you think Dad can drive you?"

"He's in the office," I remind her.

Mom looks from her work computer to me and back again. "Can we do it tomorrow?"

No, we can't! I want to scream. I *need* to wear the Gamer Girls merch for my stream with Mel White at noon, and Mom promised it would be today.

I don't mean to sound ungrateful or anything. Mom is a first-generation American and Dad moved here when he was small; I know how hard they work to afford our house and everything else. But c'mon! She *promised* we could pick up the merch today. If I don't wear Gamer Girls stuff on the stream, my friends will be disappointed because that was kind of the whole point of it. Not to mention *I'll* be disappointed, because I've really been looking forward to this.

"Do you think any of the other girls' parents can drive you?" Mom asks. "Here's the manufacturer's address. Ask for a woman named **Lottie** and say you're my daughter." She writes the manufacturer's address on a business card and slips it to me.

I take the business card and sigh. I'm used to my parents working a lot and taking meetings late, but recently, it's been way too much. Mom returns to her desk, and not unlike my attempts at *Alienlord*, I know this is a battle I've lost.

I text the Gamer Girls group chat.

Anyone around? I need a ride to the merch manufacturer. Shouldn't be too far, but too far to walk.

Since no one replies immediately, I return to my room and to *Monster Village*, which is calming, but less calming than it was before I talked to Mom.

When the group chat text messages roll in, Lucy's and Jess's parents are busy (I forgot that Jess being busy is why we had to move the Gamer Girls meeting to yesterday), but Nat and Dylan agree to pick me up. That's another good thing about Dylan being an adult—she can drive! I text Mom to let her know that I found my ride and beeline out of the house, where I see Dylan's car already waiting for me.

"Thank you so much for the ride," I say. "Mom's tied up with work stuff and—"

"Don't sweat it," replies Dylan. "You're helping *me* out on Sunday with Francis, remember?"

"Well, I just wanted to say thank you," I say.

"Again, no sweat. I looked up the location for the manufacturer, and it's right by the pet store, so I was thinking of running in and seeing if they have any discounted toys or cleaning supplies. You'd never believe how quick we go through them at the shelter."

I know they're not real pets or anything, but I kind of understand what she means. My creatures in *Monster Village* take SO much work!

After a few minutes, Dylan pulls her car into the parking lot and we all spill out. Dylan heads into the pet store while Nat and I walk to the manufacturer in the opposite direction.

The manufacturer is a small business called Lottie's Garments, and according to Mom, it's where she gets all her fundraising things done, like Relay for Life T-shirts and even beach towels with her company's name embroidered on them. Manufacturers are often overseas, but Mom likes using Lottie's Garments since it's so close. They're not the cheapest, and the prototypes were pretty much all *this* week's allowance, but what you save in shipping time is worth a lot. Especially since I need the merch for Mel White's stream tomorrow!

When Nat and I file in, I notice the Lottie's Garments storefront is packed with T-shirts, tote bags, fleece sweaters, you name it. Nat and I are careful to avoid stray thimbles and scissors on the ground, which are presumably for more customizing. I imagine myself here, having a fun time building creations for people. This is basically real-life *Monster Village* sewing!

At the helm of the storefront is a tiny woman whose hair is wrapped in a tight bun. She has a wrinkled face, but there's something kind in her eyes. I realize she reminds me a little of Abuelita, and I smile.

"Hi!" I say to the woman. "My name is Celia Gomez, and I'm here to pick up the Gamer Girls merchandise. It should be under my mom's name, Carolina Gomez."

"Celia! Of course," the woman says. "Your mom is one of my favorite customers. I was beginning to worry that something happened, since she said she'd be here in the afternoon. Is she okay?"

"She's fine. It's just work stuff," I shrug. I hope no one notices the bitterness in my voice as I say "work."

The woman—who later introduces herself as *the* Lottie of Lottie's Garments—disappears into a back corner of the room, which if you told me was just an entrance to Narnia, I would've probably believed you. Then she returns with a hat and a T-shirt.

I can hardly believe it! These are my designs, come to real life! As bummed as I am that Mom isn't here to relish in the moment, I'm grateful to have Nat by my side. And I think Nat's happy about it too because she can get her T-shirt ASAP.

Lottie unfolds the T-shirt and places it on a glass counter. Just like I imagined, it says **GAMER GIRLS** emblazoned on it, updated to have a mix of some cheetah print letters, some polka dot letters, and a console all around it. I instantly love it.

The hat is *also* gorgeous. I put it on my head and feel like a queen who's just been given a crown. Like I said, I've made jewelry before, but textile items are just different!

"Oh, Lottie, I love it!" I say. "Thank you so much!" I look back at the glass counter to grab Nat's hat and shirt too, but see there's nothing else there. Only one set. "Where's the rest?"

"The rest?" Lottie asks.

"Yes, there should be four sets of everything. So that we can approve and make more merchandise to sell," I explain.

Lottie shakes her head.

"I'm sorry, Celia. Your mom asked for a prototype, and this is it. I don't have four of each, just the one. If you like it, it'll take another two to three weeks for the extras. I hope that's okay."

Two to three weeks*?!* No, this can't be right!

"My mom promised it would all be ready—"

"She can give us a call later to confirm, but right now, that's our current schedule," Lottie says.

Nat grabs my hand and gives it a squeeze. I know Nat has anxiety, so I think she's trying to help steady me too. But I can't believe it. This is just another instance where Mom dropped the ball.

"It's okay, we'll get them later," Nat tells me. "What's important is you have yours. And it looks great."

"I just feel horrible I dragged you out here for nothing," I reply.

"I got to see where the magic happens. Besides, you're like the **best designer ever**. I can wait two weeks. It will be okay."

At least Nat is taking this well . . .

I thank Lottie anyway for the prototypes and sign a form verifying that they're approved by me. Nat doesn't say anything else. I realize that she'll never admit it to me, she's disappointed. I imagine myself in her place, and I'd be disappointed too.

Lottie bags the prototype hat and T-shirt into a canvas bag and hands it to me. I'll have the one set for Mel White's channel, at least, but nothing else.

I feel like a total failure.

CHAPTER TWELVE

When I get home from the manufacturer, it's almost eight o'clock, and Mom has *just* finished work. As she emerges from her office-cave, I'm ready to yell that she didn't order the four prototypes like we promised. But she looks so haggard, I feel kind of bad.

Mom notices that I'm upset, though.

"What's wrong?" she asks.

I take a deep breath.

"Nat and I went to pick up the merch today, and it looks *awesome*, but it wasn't all there," I tell her. "There was only one set when I asked for four."

I see Mom's face fall.

"You didn't ask for four sets, did you, Mom?"

I watch as Mom's expression turns even more crestfallen and sad.

"Cece, I'm sorry. I must have defaulted the order to what we do at work, which is one set," Mom admits.

I shake my head. Honestly, nothing will fix this, unless Mom knows of a place to get the merch even *faster*. But I also feel a little bratty admitting this—after all, it's not like Mom has been doing nothing.

"Maybe we can do a little art project together? Make some Gamer Girls *unofficial* merch?" Mom suggests. I think back to the tie-dye and puffy paint shirts we made in third grade for the school dance performance. They were cute, but we need something more *professional*. Something more Mel White–worthy.

"It's fine," I sigh. "Just . . . forget about it."

"I really want to make it up to you."

"Then don't . . . work so much," I say through my teeth. As I murmur the words, guilt overtakes me. I know Mom—and Dad—are trying to build a nice life for us, and they have succeeded. But when they aren't around all the time . . . it stings.

"When Dad and I are done with our projects, you're in for a big treat," Mom promises. "Anything you like. Promise."

"Pinky swear?"

"Pinky swear."

Mom and I lock pinkies. I hope she knows she just agreed to the next Broadway show I want to see.

Dad walks in the door not too long after with an armful of the tacos that we rain-checked earlier this week. Although I love El Cocinero, it just doesn't have the same sparkle it usually does.

The next day is **Mel White's livestream**. If I was nervous before, I'm sweating buckets now. I try to think about what my drama teacher, Ms. Czarneki, would say.

"Passion! Drive! Let the arts take the lead! Fill your heart with art and your audience will follow!"

I do a vocal warm-up—"many mumbling mice are making midnight music in the moonlight"—and take a deep breath.

Since it's a Saturday, Mom drives me over to Mel White's. I'm still a little bitter from the manufacturer fiasco, so even though I'm trying not to be angry, we travel most of the way in silence. Mom tells me a bit about the project she's working on, but I focus on the music on the radio. If I focus on the music, then I'm not focused on the livestream *or* Mom.

When we arrive at the house on the far side of

town, I exit the car with trepidation. I haven't been to this new house yet—why would I?—but Nat and Lucy were here for a party not too long ago, and they talked a little about how nice it was.

Mel White used to live next to Nat. Nat's house—and Mel White's old one—were always bigger than mine. Our houses never made me feel bad or anything, that's just the way it was. Knowing that Mel White's house now is even *nicer* makes me feel strange. And for good reason—as I traipse up the pavement, I feel like I'm walking into some sort of palace. Even at the front door, there are beautiful potted plants in ceramic pots with intricate designs on them and all the bushes and trees around the house are landscaped to look neat.

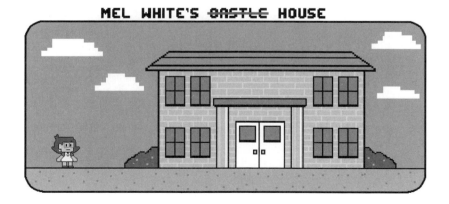

MEL WHITE'S ~~CASTLE~~ HOUSE

I ring the bell nervously and Mel White's mom answers with a smile. She's wearing an all-white track suit, and her hair with chunky highlights is styled up in a big ponytail. I don't see any makeup on her; she just has naturally nice skin. She also has two big gold hoop earrings hanging from her ears and on her feet are black slippers that I recognize as one of the newest styles from Kain East's brand.

"Celia! Welcome to our home. Mel was just talking about you," her mom says.

"Oh—really?" I reply. I wonder what she was saying. I carefully take off my shoes before entering.

"Of course! Mel's really excited to have you help her with her channel," her mom says. "I've heard you're just the expert she's been looking for. Do you need anything before the stream? Water? Juice? Fruit? Chips? Seltzer?"

Mel White's mom is almost *too* nice, just like her daughter. It's probably where she gets it from.

"Water would be great, actually," I say.

"Of course!" Her mom smiles again. "You can go up to Mel's room. It's the first door on the left. I'll be right there with some waters."

I climb the stairs cautiously, my bag swinging against my legs. Today, I've added some LTS pins and some kawaii frog pins to the bag, which feels very *Monster Village*. I haven't bought any *Monster Village* merch yet because my allowance keeps getting eaten up by other things, but I've bookmarked about a hundred things I want. I wonder if Mel gets allowance.

Mel White opens the door for me and I step inside. I take it all in. The first thing I notice is that she has a setup similar to what we have in the Gamer Girls' Den, but times *fifty*. There's a big ring light set up across from her computer, a super-neat desk, a huge stack of magazines, and a bunch of makeup products arranged on a clear acrylic swivel tray.

Everything around her computer is perfectly situated to look like it's a magazine shoot. The white shelves are filled with books and trinkets, and her bed is nicely made with one lone stuffed animal (a panda bear). I smile, thinking about my own room that's teeming with a ton of super squishy, marshmallow-like stuffed animals.

Mel White's chair is a tall blue one. It looks less like the gaming chair that Nat has and more like a regular office chair, but it's far from boring. **"MEL"** is spelled out on the back of the chair in glittering rhinestones. And Mel White herself, of course, looks just as perfect as her room and setup. She's wearing some new Jurimei earrings and a new black and white designer sweater that I saw last week in an ad. I didn't even think that sweater had come out yet, but I suppose if anyone were to have it, it would be Mel White.

"Wow, this is an amazing setup," I say.

"Thank you!" Mel White replies. She looks extra chipper today. "That reminds me. I was thinking. Maybe we can just have you game while I talk about the makeup and stuff I have? You can turn your laptop around and show the camera what you're doing every so often."

Huh? No live port to the game? That's not like the streaming the Gamer Girls do at all!

"Don't you have a way to hook things up, so people can watch me game when they tune into your channel?" I ask. "In gaming streams, you see the gamer's whole screen. That's how we do it with Gamer Girls."

The moment I ask the question, I realize I don't know why I said anything. Of course Mel White doesn't have any specific equipment, like a cord or an extra monitor or even a headset. She's not a gamer.

I shake my head, as if taking back my words.

"Never mind. I can just play in the background and show my stuff while you talk," I decide, taking my laptop out of the bag.

Mel White smiles back. She's too nice to notice my harsh tone from earlier. **"Cool!"**

She starts to set up her stuff, placing her makeup around the computer and fixing her hair in the mirror before she sits down. I take a seat in the chair set up behind her—just a regular chair, nothing fancy—and start up my laptop. I look at all the small LTS stickers that I've plastered on it. I'd been so proud of them, but now, I wonder if it looks silly and childish compared to this grown-up room and vibe.

"Okay, so here's how it's going to work. I'll introduce myself—not that I need to, obviously, but it's always nice to remind my channel who they're watching," Mel White says through her ultra-shiny teeth. "And then you'll introduce yourself. I'll show off all the makeup and you can play. I think you add a nice amount of authenticity to *Monster Village*, and my viewers will be happy to see it."

"Okay," I agree. I'm trying not to let the show get to me. *Pretend you're Ms. Czarneki*, I remind myself.

Her mom walks in two minutes later with water, which is good, because I was starting to get thirsty. The ice cubes she has are in the shape of flowers, and I think that's a cute touch I've never seen before. I make a mental note to check and see if I can customize ice in my *Monster Village* game.

And then . . . it's showtime!

"Hi, everyone! I hope you're all having a great Saturday!" Mel White's cheerful voice projects easily out of her mouth and around the room as she welcomes people to her channel. "I'm Mel, and welcome to my channel—Mel's Mirror! As you know, I always talk about the *best* and most up-to-date makeup and fashion. Today is a super-special show that I'm excited about. We'll be doing an *exclusive reveal* of the cool new *Monster Village*–inspired makeup that's coming out next month." She pauses for effect, I assume, to let people comment because I can already see people typing in the small corner of the screen. Some of them even have blue checkmarks, which means they're famous or important.

"I was honored to be sent some free samples from MegaBox Studioz. Thank you, **MegaBox!**"

I sit behind her smiling, mostly because I know I can partially be seen on camera. I want to look like I belong. I'm not sure I'm succeeding. But I make sure to stand up straight, so everyone can see my Gamer Girls T-shirt, and play nice.

"And today I even have a special guest with me," Mel White continues. "You might know her from her cool designs on *Monster Village*, or maybe because we go to the same middle school, but she's going to game right next to me while I try out all my cool new makeup. Hi, Celia! Welcome to the show!"

Mel White moves out of the way just enough so that I know everyone can fully see my face.

"Uh, hi! Hi, everyone!" I smile, trying not to feel intimidated. I know I'm speaking to a large crowd, but it's disconcerting not knowing *how* big your crowd is. "As you just heard, my name is Celia. I *love* playing *Monster Village*. Usually, I stream with the Gamer Girls, but today, I'm excited to be with you all."

I tip my hat, showing off the Gamer Girls logo. And Mel White, ever the nicest person, types and pins the Gamer Girls' channel link into the chat, so if anyone wants, they can follow us there. Pinning links is important because if someone joins the stream later, they can still click the URL, since it's **pinned** on top of the chat.

Then she once again makes herself center stage. "So first, I'm going to show you all this new lipstick. It's called Blush Tint Ruby Red. I think the ruby part is named after one of the gems you can get when you get enough stars for your town to be popular—that's what it looks like on the packaging. Right, Celia?" She waves a very fancy looking box of lipstick in front of the camera.

"Correct," I reply. "The Ruby Red gemstone is one of the rarest in the game. And I have two." I swivel my laptop around, showing off my rubies in my virtual ita bag. Mel White whoops and cheers.

Then she takes the lipstick out and slowly shows it from all angles. Mel White drags the lipstick over her mouth, pursing her lips and winking at the screen.

I can finally understand why she has so many followers. She's really good at makeup. What's more important, she also puts in the time to learn things. I'm a little impressed she knew what the game's gemstones are, especially because I'm not sure I got to that point in my demo with Nat.

"This isn't bad," Mel White decides after a moment of checking herself out. "It's a little more opaque than it looks from the color on the box, but it's got a nice ruby tint. More matte than lip oil, which I know some of you will be stoked about."

"I can design some makeup in my town too," I interject suddenly.

Mel White turns around. If she's annoyed that I

interrupted, she doesn't show it. I go on.

"So, if you come up with your own makeup design, you can lay it on the monsters' faces, and they wear makeup too," I explain. "That's why my raccoon-cat, Mapache Gato, has such a unique face. I gave him eyeliner. I also have a nail salon in my village," I continue, sharing the pixels on my laptop. "I made sure that all the different colors and symbols for nail polish match the aesthetic of my village. It took a lot of work, but that's the fun of **customizing**."

I've always had good ideas for projects and stuff, but I've never really been a "take charge" person— that's more Jess or even Nat. I can tell Mel White is surprised at the way I'm starting to control the stream, but she seems to be into it.

"Whoa, that's so cool, Celia. Well that leads me into . . ." She pauses dramatically. "The Heart of Gold Blush! It has a nice shimmery color, and you can wear it on a nice hot day to add some sparkles to your everyday look."

"Speaking of sparkles, I made a new wallpaper for one of the houses in my village," I add. "It's supposed to look like the night sky, and I made the colors all pastel, so it looks like it glows in the dark!"

I lean back again as Mel White once again takes over, showing off her products and continuing to brag about everything she's gotten to try out. This continues for about an hour, and I keep playing. I pipe up a few times to tell her that the makeup looks great. This whole setup feels strange.

At the end of the stream, Mel White gathers all her samples and holds them up in front of the camera.

"Well, that's all the time we have for today," she says cheerily. "Thanks for joining me—especially you, Farrah Grace and Patrina North! And thank you to Celia for playing *Monster Village* and showing her awesome work! If you preorder any of these makeup products, feel free to use the code MEL10 to get ten percent off. And don't forget to follow Celia and her gamer gal friends."

Mel White pulls me into an awkward hug. It actually looks seamless on camera, like she really knows what she's doing, but I've never hugged Mel White before, so it feels kind of strange. Then she shuts the livestream off.

Once she's sure the stream is done and cameras

haven't glitched, Mel White turns to me with excited eyes. "Farrah and Patrina are my mom's friends. They work with her in the city. My mom told them about my channel, and they said they would try to watch and see if they could find any **special influencers** to sponsor me! It's really exciting they tuned into this one, so thank you, Cece!"

"Cece" is usually a nickname that's reserved for my friends, but I let it slide. I guess Mel White is kind of my friend now.

"You were great, by the way," she says. "Thanks for coming and playing. It was fun!"

"Thank you! Although, it's just a lot of practice,"

I answer, gathering up my things. I share a smile with Mel White. We may be interested in different things, but she actually reminds me a bit of Nat and her streaming goals.

I pick up my phone and send my mom a quick text saying I'm done with the stream. Mom doesn't reply, though, so I make some small talk.

"Don't you have friends that play games too?" I ask curiously.

"Some of them," she replies with a shrug. "But I don't really talk to them about it."

"Maybe you should," I offer. "I mean, it's always fun to learn about other things people are doing. Especially from your **crew**."

Speaking of crew . . . I look down at my phone, hoping to see some text messages from Nat, Lucy, or Jess, but there's nothing. It's like my phone was on airplane mode, nobody's texted or messaged me at all.

"That reminds me," Mel White says, breaking into my thoughts. "You designed your shirts, right? And the hat?" I nod. "Maybe you'd want to design something for me?" she asks. "My dad was originally supposed to help out with the merch, but since Mom got remarried, he's been a bit more distant . . ."

Huh. I knew that Mel White's mom remarried and that's why they moved, but I never figured there might be more to the story there. I also never thought about designing fashion for *other people*. And now that I know how Mel White works a bit more, I figure this can't hurt. We run our livestreams very differently, but if anyone understands sometimes-distant parents, it's me. And besides, the *Monster Village* makeup sets she gave me as payment are nice. It would be kind of cool to get some more makeup.

I don't think twice about it.

"Sure," I reply.

CHAPTER THIRTEEN

Mom texts me ten minutes later to say she's running errands and Dad is grocery shopping. I guess it makes sense they're out now since they've both been so busy at work during the week (and I *have* noticed the fridge is a little empty), but I do wish one of them could come pick me up. Thankfully, Mel White's mom offers to drive me home and I accept. Her mom tells me to call her Claire, which is always cool when adults let you call them by their first name. Mom and Dad still make Nat and Jess call them Mr. and Mrs. Gomez.

Claire has a big SUV with plush leather seats and a lavender air freshener. I climb into the front seat and buckle my seatbelt.

"Thanks for driving me," I say. Mel White stayed back at the house, so it's just me and her mom.

"Anytime," replies Claire. "How'd it go? Do you think you'll be coming over more?"

"I dunno," I reply. "I mean, it was a lot of fun. I'm just not sure when I'll be back. I might be making your daughter some T-shirts, but we'll see. She is very professional. It's impressive."

Claire chuckles.

"Mel has been professional since she was little," she replies. "And always obsessed with makeup. I used to come out of a shower and find my two-year-old smearing lipstick everywhere. I had to store my stuff in a locker until she was ten." She changes lanes. "I know my daughter likes pretending to be this **ethereal princess boss queen**, but she also has her weak points, just like everyone else. I think she can really benefit from having a friend like you."

Mel White's *friend*? The statement feels so strange to me. Mel White has always been this entity—this first name, last name kind of person who I could never quite place in my life. But now that we've hung out, I can see what Claire means. There's a lot more to Mel than meets the eye, and a lot more that I haven't seen. I think about her comments about her dad. I'm grateful that I see my parents every day. Even if it's not for long, I can't imagine not seeing one of them during the week.

Claire pulls into my driveway and watches as I get out. I've never thought my house was small, but after seeing Mel's, I see just how tiny it is.

After hanging out at home and finishing some more *Monster Village* designs for the contest, I see an incoming group call from the Gamer Girls. I pick up immediately, hoping we can talk about Mel's livestream.

"How was it?" Jess says first thing.

"OMG tell us *everything*," rings Nat.

"What's Mel's video setup like? Does she have a fancy camera?" asks Lucy.

Although all the Gamer Girls answer on their own phones, I notice an echo in each one. I wonder if they're all together at someone's house, or somewhere else. I can't exactly be mad that they were spending time without me. After all, I was the one who spent the day without *them*. But it does sting a little that I wasn't at least told about it.

"You saw it, right?" I cut in. I don't mean to be rude; they're just acting like they didn't watch at all.

"Well . . . no," Lucy admits. I can hear the guilt in her voice. "But we knew you'd tell us all about it!"

I bristle a bit at the word "we." *We*, as though *I* am not a part of it.

I know I'm being silly, but c'mon. Where are my supportive besties?

"It was fine," I admit, a bit shorter than I intended. "I mean, Mel sat there and went through all her stuff and talked to her channel. I was sitting behind her, and

I played *Monster Village*. Plus, I wore the merch, and Mel popped our livestream link into her chat. Oh, and I agreed to make her some merch."

If I've learned anything, it's come out with the truth, ASAP.

"But . . . you're finishing *our* merch first, right?" Lucy asks. I can tell she's a little hesitant about the idea of me making Mel merch too. We don't have competing streams by any means, but you don't want your designer spread too thin!

"Duh," I say, and that's that.

I can tell the Gamer Girls are waiting for some juicy gossip, maybe about Mel or her room or her friends, but I don't really have that. I mean, I didn't go over there trying to spy on her or anything. And honestly, Mel is like us in a lot of ways. Sure, she has money and spends a ton of time on her hair. But she isn't *that* different. I spend a lot of time on my game! So does everyone else.

"Alright," Nat says with a heavy sigh. "Now that means we can get back to the important things. Like our *own* gaming!"

I bristle at that. The way Nat said our *own*

gaming . . . as if I didn't game on my *own* . . . maybe it's all in my head.

"Okay, have fun," I say, and hang up. I don't ask them where they are. Something tells me I'll feel better if I don't know.

When Dad comes back from the grocery store on Saturday night, he's gotten all the items needed to make pozole rojo. Dad asks me to help cook it, and I add a **dash of cinnamon**—my signature trick—before serving it to us. I'm still a little bitter that my parents haven't been available much, but I know they're doing it for all of us, so I try to bite my tongue (but not with hot stew!).

On Sunday, Nat texts us and says that we don't need to watch Francis anymore because Marc has the flu. I'm not too bummed. I only have seven and a half more days for the MegaBox Studioz contest, which means it's time to *bring it*. So I spend the whole day working on my village, and it's looking snazzy, if I do say so myself.

On Monday at school, I run up to Jess, Lucy, and Nat at our usual spot. Nat gives out the morning treats, which today are honey clusters with drizzled chocolate on top.

"I mffs howf food thef arf," I say, as I shove the food in my mouth.

Jess laughs. "Come again?"

I swallow. "I forgot how good these are."

Lucy giggles. Her long hair swings back and forth. We make our way from the usual meeting place to inside the school. I still have some honey cluster in my mouth when a gaggle of people saunters up to us.

"Oh em gee!"

"Look! It's her! *The* gamer!"

I smile at Nat. Is it finally happening? Is Nat going to be a **famous streamer**? I knew she and Lucy were locked in a battle last night, but it must have been *super* epic to elicit this kind of response.

"That's the one who has the cool town and does all the designs!"

A girl with pigtails points at me. Nat's on my left, so I do a double-take just to confirm.

Me?

A few girls, including Brooke and Jenn—who are also friends with Mel—walk toward me excitedly.

"Your stream was *awesome*!" Brooke says excitedly as she approaches.

I freeze-panic. Since my own friends hadn't watched Mel's stream, I hardly expected anyone else to. But here are some middle school girls, pointing at me from the crowd!

"My—oh, yeah, well . . ." I trail off, fumbling for words. "It wasn't my stream. It was Mel's video. I usually stream—"

"I can't believe you made all those!" Jenn cuts in. "All those designs and everything! I've never seen anything so cool! How did you do it all?"

I'm not sure what to say. I'm used to people commenting on our streams when we get together and game, telling us what they like. But it's a little different when people are saying it *in real life*. And at school!

"My friends play too," I offer, trying to point to include them in the conversation. "They're *really* good at gaming. We actually play all together on our channel. We're the Gamer Girls."

"Yeah, but you're the one who's made all the cool stuff for *Monster Village*," Brooke says impatiently, as if I don't get why they only want to talk to *me*. I smile, but my stomach is churning now. It feels weird to be the center of attention like this, especially when my friends aren't getting acknowledged too. I know I wanted to show off and feel important, but I didn't know it would feel this weird to get the spotlight!

"We saw you on Mel's stream, you showed off your whole town," Jenn says, pulling at her hair excitedly. "And I can't even *believe* you did all that stuff. You're so talented! You must have practiced *forever* and spent so much time getting things right."

"I just play a lot after school," I answer, which is the truth. I'm hugely aware of my friends, who are still standing behind me. I hope they don't mind.

"Well, we think you're **awesome**," Jenn says. "I want to watch you play all the time. I'm going to start playing *Monster Village* now so I can try to use your designs and make some myself!"

Huh? Jenn is going to play *Monster Village*?

Nat and Lucy mentioned that Brooke and Jenn have Major 6 consoles—that's another reason I told Mel to play with her friends—but since my own friends were uninterested in *Monster Village*, I assumed everyone else kind of would be too.

"That's . . . great!" I say with a smile because that *does* make me happy. The fact that Jenn wants to play

Monster Village because I inspired her? Inspiring girl gamers is exactly what we all dreamed of when we started our group!

"Anyway, I'm heading to class now, but I'll get your number from Mel, and text you about visiting your village later this week. See ya!" Brooke says. Then she swiftly walks away.

I turn toward my friends to make a funny jest to them, but they've walked away too. Then the second bell rings and I know I have to book it.

I don't talk about what happened in the hallway for the rest of the day. I feel like I can't. Am I a bad friend? Did I sabotage Nat's dream?

At lunch, we don't talk about anything that's happened either. But we also don't talk much about anything. Jess regales us about her soccer practice; I can see that Nat isn't super interested. I focus on today's lunch—veggie patties with chef salad—and try to spear the cherry tomatoes with my spork.

After classes are over, I notice that Jess leaves

quickly for her track meet and Lucy and Nat mumble something about getting picked up together. Usually, I take the bus home, but it's only after they leave that I remember Mom is picking me up too, so we can go to Abuelita's house for dinner. I'm almost late because of it, rushing out of the building and finding my mom's car idling in the parking lot.

"Sorry, sorry, sorry!" I shove myself into the car and kick my backpack to the floor. "I got uh . . . caught up talking with my friends."

Mom sighs. "It's okay. I just hope that we don't hit rush hour traffic driving to Philadelphia."

"Ugh, I *hope* not," I groan.

"How was school?" Mom asks.

"Fine." I bite down on my lip. "Um, I guess a lot of people saw me and Mel playing on her channel together over the weekend."

"Oh, really?" Mom flicks on her blinker. "That's great! Didn't you say she has a big following with her makeup channel?"

"Yeah, but I didn't, like, expect people to pay attention," I admit. "I mean, they were there to see *her*. I was just there to play my game."

"Well, I guess people did pay attention," Mom says, before she pauses. "Celia, I know your dad and I haven't been around much lately, but I'm glad you found something outside of art that you like to do."

"It's still art," I insist. "It's **designing**."

"Well, just make sure all that *designing* doesn't interfere with your schoolwork," Mom says pointedly, giving me a look out of the corner of her eye.

Thankfully, the rest of the trip goes by fairly quickly, even with some annoying traffic. When we reach Abuelita's house, I stretch my legs before walking to the door and opening it. Abuelita's house is a cute little place, but Abuelita doesn't need much anyway, so it's perfect for her.

"Hi, Abuelita!" I say when I enter, looking at the photos on the walls. There are a lot of pictures of me from school over the years and some photos of my parents on their wedding day.

Abuelita is sitting on the couch, reading a book. When I walk in, she looks up and smiles.

"I was *wondering* when you'd show up," she says.

"Sorry, there was traffic," I reply as Mom walks in behind me. "And we left late because I kiiiiinda got distracted at school. But we're here and ready to eat some dinner!"

"Good," Abuelita answers. Meanwhile, Mom walks into the kitchen to help prepare the food she's brought. Mom always brings dinner to either make or heat up. It's just easier, and Abuelita always appreciates it.

"How's school? Okay?"

"Yeah, okay," I answer cheerily—cheerily enough that hopefully she won't press me about it.

"And your games? Did you tell your friends about that thing you were worried about?"

I should've known Abuelita would remember our conversation from before. She pays too much attention to things when we talk. But at least I have an answer for that.

"I did tell them. And guess what? They weren't mad!" I reply. I may have my doubts over what happened today, but *that*, at least, is old news.

"That's great," Abuelita says. "So, there was nothing to worry about."

Hmm. Well that's the thing—even though I didn't fill Abuelita in, nothing *is* wrong about being good at something or getting recognized for it! But somehow,

I've felt like it's *wrong* for me to be good at *Monster Village* because I'm not a gamer. Not in the **Nat-Lucy sense**, anyway.

"Anyway, it's fine," I continue. "I promise. Also, you should watch our next Gamer Girls stream. If you do, I'll give you a special shoutout."

Abuelita laughs. "How can I watch?" she asks.

"I'll figure out how to do it from your phone," I say. "You just have to create a username and go to the channel—and subscribe, of course—here, I'll show you right now!"

Abuelita holds out her phone and I take it from her. I start busily working, putting in the web address for our streaming page in her mobile browser and then creating an account with her email so she can log in. I make sure to save everything and bookmark it, especially our channel.

"You're all set," I say after a few moments, handing Abuelita her phone back. "Now you can watch me game. All you have to do is go to the page on Friday nights and it should be automatic."

Abuelita laughs. "Okay, I'll try to remember," she promises. "What would I do without you?"

"I don't know, but you *definitely* wouldn't know as much about cool video games," I say with a smile. Then Mom serves us dinner, reheated of course, and all seems well with the world.

CHAPTER FOURTEEN

The next morning is a Tuesday, and things are normal at school—or relatively normal. Nat hands out some blueberry muffins. They're Lucy's favorite, and she savors hers. I notice that Nat is making less eye contact with me than usual, but I figure that must be me imagining things.

While walking to Ms. Kenshaw's math class, a floppy-haired boy waves to me in the hallway.

"Hey, you're Celia, right?" he says.

I stop in my tracks. Okay, it's not just any floppy-haired boy. It's Liam Porter.

The Liam Porter. Who is not important.

"Um, hi," I say.

"I watched your stream with Mel. It was awesome," he says casually.

I feel my face get hot and I wonder if Liam can tell.

"Thank you! Do you watch Mel's channel often?" I

ask. I can't imagine Liam Porter needing to know the latest in makeup (some boys at our school *do* wear makeup, and that's cool, but I don't think Liam is one of those boys).

"Nah. I wanted to catch it for you, though. I heard you're really crushing it in *Monster Village*," Liam says and smiles.

"Will you be on the stream again?" Liam asks. "Or maybe do a solo stream? I think that would be better for you. Less . . . noise."

A *solo* stream? Of everything anyone has said this week, a *solo stream* is the most terrifying. I'd never considered doing a solo stream of *Monster Village*, and honestly, I don't even want to. I want to game with my friends, not do this all on my lonesome! But somehow, when Liam says it, the idea doesn't sound too absurd.

"Hmm. Well, I usually stream with the Gamer Girls on Fridays. You should check it out," I say.

"Oh, yeah. Nat and Lucy are cool too," he says. "And Jess. She saved my butt in history class."

I laugh. "Jess *always* saves my butt," I reply. As I say "**my butt**," I feel my face get a little red.

The fourth period bell rings.

"Well, catch ya later, Celia Gomez," he says, before speeding off.

I stand a moment in the hallway, recounting what just happened.

Oh em gee!

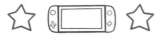

After I get home from school, Mom and Dad are cooped up in their offices (typical). Mom's left out some more yuca chips on the counter, so I grab a handful before checking my phone.

When I do check my phone, I see a text from Nat.

Need help with Dylan's dog, Nat types. *He's driving me NUTS!*

I see that she's texted just me, not the group chat. I wonder why Nat is singling me out, but I don't question it too much.

Dad's in an audio-only meeting, so he drives me over to Dylan's, all the while his phone is on speaker. I listen to the meeting and it's pretty boring. Skyscraper this, projection that. I know there must be a lot of security clearances for building actual skyscrapers, so this is important, but *Monster Village* makes building seem so easy.

When I get to Dylan's place, Nat answers the door looking frazzled, her face strawberry red, as if she's been screaming.

"Uh . . . things aren't going so well, I guess?" I ask I walk inside and close the door. Inside, a moderate section of the apartment has been blocked off with a dog gate, but there are treats scattered all over the floor and one of Dylan's chairs looks super chewed on.

"I don't know why he won't listen," Nat says in frustration. "He was *so good* when Dylan was here.

And the moment she left, everything became chaotic! This is harder than defeating aliens."

I can't help but laugh, because of course Nat would compare watching her sister's dog to **defeating aliens** in a video game. Nat looks annoyed.

"It's not *funny*, Celia!" she interjects.

"I know, I'm sorry," I apologize, making myself serious again. "But I thought you wanted to help."

"I do!" Nat says. "I didn't expect it to be so *hard*!"

"I dunno, sometimes things are hard," I say.

As if responding to us, Francis barks loudly. Nat holds her hand up in a command. "Be quiet . . . sit . . . stay!" she instructs, moving her hand in different motions that I guess mean something in Dog. Francis looks like he wants to protest, but he slumps to the floor after a few seconds.

I decide that with Francis quiet, maybe now is a good time to get Nat's mind off her current annoyance.

"Um, so that contest for *Monster Village* ends on Sunday," I say. "Maybe at this week's Gamer Girls meeting, I could stream my village again. Like, stream the process or something. So many people watched when I played with Mel!"

"Yeah, yeah, I know," Nat says coldly. Is that . . . bitterness I detect?

"It proves people are still interested, at least," I say, trying not to let her tone get to me.

"I guess," Nat says, avoiding my eyes. "But we don't have to do something just because it's popular. Besides, it's Jess's turn to pick the game."

That might be true, but I wish Nat could be excited for the contest anyway.

While Nat prepares Francis's food, I sit down and start *Monster Village* on my laptop, pulling up my town. After a little bit, Nat comes back with a bowl full of food. Then I hear Jess and Lucy arriving. I didn't realize they were coming too, but I guess it makes sense that Nat invited them. It's strange she sent out individual texts, though, and I'm starting to wonder if she sent them out to the group of three, and me individually. But I push that from my brain. It's not us or them. It's just us!

"I was thinking we could get some practice in," Lucy says when we're all settled, sounding excited. "I'm ready to kick some butt!"

Maybe I should say something before we start. It's

now or never, right? If I don't say anything, I feel like things are just going to continue to feel weird and I don't want that.

"Before we start streaming, I wanted to check in about the contest," I say.

Nat groans. "Celia, we talked about this!"

"Can you just hear me out? Why are you so anti–*Monster Village*?" I ask.

Lucy has an answer. I'm kind of shocked she does, because I thought it was more rhetorical.

"Because we're **just not good enough!**" Lucy replies, as if it's the most obvious thing in the world. "Why would we want to enter a contest for something we're not good at?"

"It doesn't matter how good you are!" I answer.

"Says someone who is *great* at the game," points out Nat.

I turn to share a look with Jess, hoping to connect on the same level that we did not too long ago in Ms. Kenshaw's class. But she just shakes her head and mouths "Switzerland." Ugh.

I decide to drop it. Liam Porter's words come back in my head. Maybe what I need to do is a solo stream, especially if my friends won't let me game on this one. Gamer Girl? That sounds kind of lonely.

I try to focus on tonight's friend hangout, but I can't. I know that Nat and Lucy battle each other in **Alienlord**, and Jess sometimes too, but it's starting to feel like we're all battling IRL. Only they're battling with alien laser swords and I'm armed with . . . a backpack. Ugh.

CHAPTER FIFTEEN

While I'm getting ready for school the next day, my phone *pings!* with a message. I look down at the text, expecting to see something from Nat, Lucy, or Jess. Instead, I'm surprised to see a new message from Mel.

Hey!! Guess what? I got some more new makeup in. Wanna come over and play again? Alsooooo . . . any updates on those merch designs?

I've been so busy with my own things, I forgot about the merch I promised that I'd design for Mel. I'm sure I can have something worked up by this afternoon though—that is, if Ms. Kenshaw doesn't call on me in math class. But I also know that if I don't have our own merch ready first, the Gamer Girls will have my head.

I speed downstairs, where Mom is making her daily pot of coffee.

"Any idea on when Lottie will have the rest of my

merch in?" I ask her. "She said two weeks, but maybe it can be sooner?"

Mom's face falls.

"Oh. I'll call later this week. I'm sorry, it must have slipped my mind," she says, as she adds some creamer to her cup.

I'm feeling annoyed. I really haven't asked Mom for much lately, and this is taking me over the edge.

"My friends are counting on me. I know I can't count on you, but please do this one thing?"

Okay, maybe my words are a bit harsh, but I must be honest, it's what I'm thinking lately. Sure, Mom drove me to Abuelita's, and sure, she tries to make sure I have a well-rounded schedule, but she hasn't been there for me much this year at school and I'm starting to really feel it. Plus, it's kind of a problem when you feel closer with your grandmother a whole state away than the mom who lives with you.

Mom's face flinches. Alright. Maybe my words were more than a bit harsh.

"Cece," Mom starts to say.

"I don't want to hear it," I reply. "I just need the designs. Now."

I turn on my heel and continue getting ready for school. It's not like Mom can say no or call me back. She doesn't want me to be late for school any more than my teachers do.

I finish getting dressed and stare at my book bag for the day. I like to change it up, like how I wore my ita bag recently, but decide that today, I'm feeling my regular Japanese-style book bag, called a randoseru. It's red and Dad got it for me when he was doing some work in Tokyo.

Mom drives me to school. She doesn't mention our earlier conversation at first until we're just a block away.

"Is everything okay, Cece?" Mom says. "I'm sorry I haven't been around . . ."

"It's fine," I snap back. "Everything's fine. I just need you to do this one thing for me, okay?"

Mom nods, understanding. I feel bad about how I'm treating her, but I know she feels bad about how she's treated me too. And I think we're at a standstill until things change, so she doesn't press.

When I get to school, Lucy, Nat, and Jess meet me at the front of the school as usual, with Nat doling out mini chocolate chip cake pops before we head inside.

MINI CHOCOLATE CHIP CAKE POPS

FOUR WHEN YOU'RE FEELING STRESSED.
GET IT?

x4

Everyone seems in good spirits. I don't sense any awkwardness from Nat, even though I'm waiting for it, and I breathe a sigh of relief as we break away for our different home rooms. But as I head down the hall, I hear a distinctive voice behind me followed by the sound of heels clacking against the floor.

"Celia!"

It's Mel.

Mel's tone is light and maybe just a *little* bossy if you listen hard enough. But I shake that thought from my brain. "Did you get my message this morning?" Mel asks softer now.

I stop and turn around, shifting my backpack against my shoulders. "Yeah," I answer. "Um, I'm sorry, I'm a little late on the merch design. But I'm working on it!"

"Cool cool," Mel says. "I got a *lot* of messages asking if you were coming back to play again because you were really good. You were such a super awesome player. Also, just so you know, if we get together, we *have* to do it on Friday night this time. That's when my mom's friends are free next, and if we're lucky, they'll set us both up with some cool fashion blogging events."

I imagine myself at Fashion Week in the city. It's always been a goal of mine.

"I get it," I say. "Let me see if there's an easy time we can change our stream to." After all, we recently changed the Gamer Girls meeting for one of Jess's track meets, so what's one more Thursday stream?

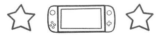

Mel's words bounce around my brain all day. When Ms. Kenshaw calls on me in math class, I almost tell her the answer is a Mel, but thankfully, Jess comes in for the save yet again. (It was a *mile*, not a Mel. I was close!)

When I get home from school, I put my stuff down and make myself a snack, sitting down at the kitchen table. After checking that Mom is locked in her office and Dad is running an errand, I pick up the phone and call Abuelita.

"Celia!" Abuelita seems surprised to hear from me when she picks up the phone. "How is everything?"

"Okay," I say, chewing on the crust of my sandwich. "Um, I'm calling because I wanted to ask your advice."

"Advice is dangerous," Abuelita says. "What if I give the wrong one?"

"You never do, Abuelita," I say back. "Even if you're sometimes out-of-touch."

I'm not sure how my joke will land, but thankfully, Abuelita chuckles.

"Well then, what did you want to talk to me about?"

I take a deep breath. "Okay," I say, steadying myself. "That girl, Mel, asked me to hang out with her again. And design some clothes for her. And I don't know if I should."

"Did you have fun last time?" Abuelita asks. Abuelita reminds me a little of Jess. They ask simple questions, but the answers aren't so simple.

"Yes. But . . ." I trail off.

Abuelita nods.

"Well, it sounds like you have an answer to your

question," she says. "You should do whatever makes you happy."

I groan. "Okay, Abuelita, I know I said it never happens, but this time your advice stinks."

Abuelita tries again. "When I was a little girl, a few of my friends were excellent chess players. We had a club, kind of like Gamer Girls. We'd play chess every day, and sometimes, I would let them win."

"Why did you do that?"

"Because if I wanted to, I would have beaten them every time I played the game," Abuelita replies. "Winning *is* super fun, but it's also not everything. Sometimes I just wanted to play chess with my friends. Of course, when they found out, they were angry with me. And jealous. It's never a good idea to lie to your friends. We didn't speak for almost a whole year until we patched things up. So, I think you need to do what's fun for you. And your friends will support you if they are good ones. Comprende?"

I sigh. "Okay, that was good advice," I admit. "But I didn't know you played chess. You'll have to teach me someday. Promise?"

"Don't be mad if you lose," Abuelita laughs.

"Deal," I answer.

We chat a little more about school before hanging up, then I take my phone out of my bag and open it. I stare at the messaging app for a long time, then pull up Mel's picture-perfect face. My response is simple.

I can come play this weekend.

Great!!! Mel immediately responds, almost too quickly. Seriously, was she waiting around for me? *Can't wait!*

I put my phone down and take another bite of my sandwich. Now that the deed is done, I know I have to ask my friends to move the Gamer Girls meeting—or figure something else out. But at least I know that I'm doing what *I* want to do. Individuals make up a group, and a group is comprised of individuals.

The next day at lunch, Lucy excitedly takes over the conversation by talking about a new headset that she wants to buy.

"And the best part is, we can keep it at Dylan's. It'll be like a **shared headset!**" she says, showing off a photo on her phone of the one she's looking at. It's hot pink and has cat-shaped ears and a big microphone attached. "My dad is going to take me to the mall after school today and I'm going to use my babysitting money to get it."

"So cute," says Jess.

"It's a great idea," Nat adds. "We can all try it out on Friday. Celia, what do you think?"

"Um," I say, figuring it's a good time to break in if I can. "I don't think I'm gonna be at the meeting this weekend. Or maybe we can move it again?"

"Oh no," Lucy says. "Is everything okay?"

"Yeah, um, well, everything's fine. I hope. See, Mel asked me to play *Monster Village* again with her," I say carefully, making sure to keep my voice casual, but I'm pretty sure I sound nervous. "Anyway, there's some big sponsors or whatever tuning in to her stream on Friday, so that's when she wants to shoot it, and I want to be there, and we moved our meeting two weeks ago for Jess, so I was hoping maybe we could make another exception."

There's a short silence among my friends. Then Nat shrugs.

"Dylan's place isn't available this Thursday," she says pointedly. "Francis is meeting with some more potential adopters, and we can't intervene."

"Oh," I reply. "Saturday?"

"Track meet," chimes Jess.

"Sunday?"

"I promised my mom that I'd help her with the garden," says Lucy.

Mayday. **MAYDAY!**

"I mean, I guess it's fine that you miss this one," Nat says finally. "Maybe we can broadcast an *Alienlord* battle, the three of us."

There we go again. *The three of us.* I hone in on the word "us." I know I'm the one saying no this week, but it still cuts like a knife.

Lucy pauses and takes a drink from her soda. "Well, I'll still get the headphones. I guess you can try out the new headphones another time, Celia."

I notice that she uses "Celia" and not "Cece," and I wonder if that's intentional.

"By the way, any update on the merch?" asks Nat.

"It hasn't been two weeks," I remind her. I don't bother mentioning that Mom also hasn't done her part to check in.

Nat was supportive earlier, but now she looks like she just chewed on a too-sour candy.

"I guess I just want to make sure our merch comes in before your work for Mel. Ha, ha!" She enunciates the *ha*'s out loud, not that she's really laughing.

We all go back to our lunch. I want to say more, but I feel like there's not really anything else for me to do, and Lucy quickly changes the subject to the games that they're going to play on Friday. I know I can't participate in the conversation since I just told them I wasn't going to be there, so I sit silently and eat my bag of chips.

CHAPTER SIXTEEN

I spend most of math class working up some designs for Mel's channel. Since Mel is very minimalist, I decide to go with a minimalist approach on her merch too, which is *way* different from what I've worked up for Gamer Girls. I've decided that shirts with pockets would be nice so you can store extra makeup in them, and I add the words *glam with me* all lowercase, in script, right above the pocket. That's her motto, even though her channel is called Mel's Mirror. I also work up an alternate design in case Mel wants a different one. This one is for a makeup carrying case, since I figure that most people who watch Mel's channel need a place to store their makeup when they're on the go.

As much as I'd love to wear my Gamer Girls merch again on Mel's channel, I can't exactly show up two weeks in a row with the same outfit, so I opt for the snapback hat only and a new set of clothes.

I don't have a lot of stuff that Mel would probably consider "super fashionable," but luckily, I *do* have a lot of cool-looking and funky garments. I choose my most **extra** pair of overalls with zebra stripes on them and pair them with a long sleeve black top. I tie up my hair in two big buns on either side and put on some of the lip gloss that Mel gave me. When I arrive downstairs, Mom gives me a look and I know she's wondering why I look more dressed up than usual. But thankfully, she doesn't say anything about it. She has something else on her brain.

"I called Lottie's Garments," Mom says. "The four sets should be ready on Monday."

I beam. That's a whole five days early!

"Oh my gosh!" I say. "Thank you, thank you!"

Like I said, I know I've been a brat, but Mom finally put in some effort, and I really appreciate that.

Mom drives me to Mel's house again. This time, I'm feeling good, so I'm a bit chattier in the car.

"Are the Gamer Girls going to Mel's too?" Mom asks curiously.

"No," I reply. "They're playing a different game on their stream today." The way I say it, it sounds so obvious. Like, of course I wouldn't come over to do something I don't want to do. And of course, they wouldn't be here, doing something they don't want to do. Friends can do different things!

"By the way, did you know Abuelita used to play chess?" I ask. Abuelita is Mom's mom, although they didn't speak for a few years before I was born. They're both very **headstrong women**, and sometimes Mom doesn't know exact details from Abuelita's life.

"She tried teaching me once, when I was a little girl," Mom smiles. "But she beat me a lot. So, I never wanted to play."

I laugh. Mom reminds me of Nat now. I wonder if the Gamer Girls would ever be into board games. I mean, games are games, right?

Mom drives me to Mel's house. It feels nice that we're getting along better now. Claire welcomes me once again with a warm smile, and I head upstairs to Mel's room, where Mel is sitting on her bed. I notice there *are* some additional lights surrounding her computer, where all her new makeup is displayed in cute little clear cases.

"Hi, Celia!" Mel smiles as she finishes putting on

lipstick. She hops off her bed. "I'm so happy you're here! This is gonna be fun!"

"It will be," I declare. I put my bag down and sit on one of the chairs that she's pulled up by her computer. "Wanna see the merch designs?"

"Do I?" Mel laughs. "Yes, yes, let's see it!"

I pull out my designs for the T-shirt and makeup case. I'm a little nervous, but I'm confident this is the aesthetic that Mel is aiming for.

Mel purses her lips. For a moment, she has a real poker face. Then she breaks out into a smile.

"This is better than I could've ever imagined, Cece!" she says.

"You like it?"

"I *love* it," Mel adds. But I see something's troubling her. She's smiling, but her eyes are saying something else.

If this were Jess, I'd poke fun at her—Jess responds well to that. If it were Nat, I'd say, "come out with it." If it were Lucy, well, it would never be Lucy, I love her, but she's a bit of a blabbermouth. Mel? I have absolutely no idea.

Mel sighs and then tries again.

"I'm sorry. It's not you. It's just—my dad was originally supposed to help me with these designs, and now I know he won't. I know I asked you to make these, and I do really appreciate it. I just wish there was something we could do together."

Weirdly enough, I connect a lot with Mel on this one. After all, *my* parents are **missing in action** pretty much all the time.

I've never admitted this to the Gamer Girls. Jess's family is close-knit; Nat's is pretty stable; I don't know Lucy's family well, but it seems the same. I *am* close with Mom and Dad, of course, but they're almost never present for a full day. In fact, I can't remember the last *full day* I ever spent with them.

"I'm lonely a lot too," I say.

Mel just looks up at me and bats her super-long eyelashes. And then, miraculously, she doesn't say anything else.

Like Abuelita, Mel knows that deep down, I won't admit anything I'm not ready to. And admitting this out loud to someone else was *huge*. But Mel doesn't bother me. Nor does she re-hash anything else she said. She straightens her back a bit and gets right to it.

See what I mean? This girl is a total professional.

"So today, I'm thinking I'll show off some purses while you game," Mel says. "Since we're trying to impress the fashion people, of course. Purses are *totes* glam." Her pun is Mom-worthy, and I grin. "Plus, they're *Monster Village*—inspired, and it even comes with a special holder for a sunscreen stick. I reapply sunscreen, like, religiously every two hours. It's the number one cause of aging."

I'll be honest. I'm thirteen. I've never thought about the number one cause of aging before. But I guess Mel has, so I just listen.

The purses are in the shapes of different colored sparkling stars, which I know is to represent the collectible stars you get for building your village. I'll be honest, they *are* cute and they're something I would carry around.

"They're amazing," I agree. "Hey, I know you don't have a way for me to plug in my game, but since the MegaBox contest is over in two days, do you think I can test out Mapache Gato Village a bit? I'd like to get some fan reaction—or not—on the final touches."

"Sure, whatever works," Mel says, sitting down and flipping her hair back. She opens her browser to pull up her channel and adjusts the camera. "Just remember to introduce yourself when you're ready." Then Mel's phone *dings!* "Oh!" she says. "Jenn and Brooke are here."

"You invited Jenn and Brooke?" I ask.

"Well, it's more like they invited themselves," Mel admits. "I said you were guest-starring again today, and they know my address, so bada bing, bada boom. They're excited to see you."

Jenn and Brooke burst into Mel's room. I've never spent much time with them either. Jenn is tall, with jet-black hair and brown eyes. She could probably be a runway model if she tried. Meanwhile, Brooke is her polar opposite—she's petite with strawberry red hair and has dazzling blue eyes.

Both girls give me a big hug, as if I'm a celebrity or something. Jenn compliments my zebra pattern and makes me do a whole 360 turnaround, so I can show off every part of my outfit. Then Brooke shows me a *Monster Village* enamel pin that she bought at a comic shop the day before. Jenn and Brooke both live in Mel's neighborhood—a.k.a, more big fancy houses—and I guess when you live in a big fancy house, you can buy whatever you want.

"Celia! I wanted to visit your village this week, and now it's finally happening," Jenn practically screeches in my ear.

"Oh my gosh, this is going to be the **most fun**," adds Brooke. She takes her phone out and grabs a selfie with all of us. And when I say "grabs," I mean "grabs." Mel poses perfectly, of course, and Jenn was already at the ready—presumably this happens a lot—but I look so startled, she has to hold me in the frame. I know they're being nice, but it just feels a bit strange.

"Okay, well, I think we have everything we need to start," I say, sitting down and getting comfortable in my seat. I prepare myself for Mel to start her recording while Jenn and Brooke huddle in the back. As I look down at the purple watch on my wrist, I realize my friends must be getting ready to go to Dylan's right now. I find myself wondering if Francis found his forever home or not, and which color Dylan's streak is today.

No, don't think about that, I tell myself. *It'll just make you sad.*

Then it's **lights, camera, action!**

"Hi, everyone!" Mel's perky, sunny voice jars me out of my thoughts. "Thanks for tuning in today again for Mel's Mirror, where you glam with me! I'm here again with superstar gamer Celia, who is playing *Monster Village!*"

I wave awkwardly in the background, trying to act natural. "It's good to be here playing again," I say, hoping that I sound as perky as Mel does. "I'll be sharing my entry for the MegaBox Studioz contest this week. I can't wait to show it to you!"

"Stoked for that," Mel says, turning the camera back toward her. "I'm also so pleased to invite my best friends, Brooke and Jenn, back to my show. You've met them on a few makeover sessions before. Everyone, say hi!" Mel points the camera to the girls in the back. They smile.

"Four girls gaming together. We love it!" Brooke says, giddy as ever.

Four girls gaming together. Okay, now I feel kind of bad. But there's nothing I can do—the camera's rolling. Seriously, though. How did I manage to be in a quartet of girls from my middle school, gaming on a stream, while my *real* best friends are at Dylan's, battling away?

Nat, Lucy, and Jess would be so upset if they saw.

You didn't know that Brooke and Jenn were coming over, and it's not like your friends are watching the stream anyway, I remind myself. *They didn't catch your first one.*

"Now let me share with you all some *awesome* purses that the *Monster Village* team sent me. I'll be honest, these aren't my typical purses of choice, okay? If anyone's a big tote bag gal like me, don't fret. You're going to have your mind blown. And just so you know, you can only order them through certain stores. But you can see them here first!"

I watch Mel show off each of the purses, holding them up so everyone can see the designs and look at the straps and the zipper. She demos the place where the sunscreen stick goes, which I guess really is important, because a bunch of commenters with blue checkmarks go nuts.

Mel then stands up and shows how the bags look while being carried around, opening them to show how much room they have inside. I realize how natural she seems in front of the camera, and I wonder if that's just Mel being Mel, or if she's learned how to specifically show off with doing so much on her channel.

I notice that Brooke and Jenn take more of a backseat than I did last time. They say things like, "wicked," "awesome," or "great," but don't offer much commentary aside from that.

"Celia, why don't you show people what you've made recently?" Mel asks, turning the camera to me.

"Sure!" I hold up my laptop so everyone can see my village, which has a big sign in front of one of the houses. "Uh, so if, hi, everyone! If you don't remember, my name is Celia, and this is Mapache Gato Village. I'm participating in the MegaBox Studioz contest this week, which means if I win, I get exclusive access to the new DLC—that means downloadable content. And my stuff would be featured on all the new *Monster Village* promos. I usually don't care about all of that, but it's important because I'm representing my friends, the **Gamer Girls**. We have a weekly stream where we game together. It's awesome."

I know my friends aren't watching, but I make sure to plug Gamer Girls just in case. I notice that Mel hasn't pinned our stream to the chat this time. Instead, it's a link to the preorder for the purses.

As I talk, I pull up some of my new buildings and some of the new game designs I've made. I quickly get to work showing them off, explaining how I had to use just the right number of pixels in the design app to create the intricate look of a woven sweater with a Dalmatian on it, so that other monsters in my village can wear it too.

Next, I sit and watch as Mel goes through all her new colors of lipstick and blush, turning to the camera and making sure to show off how each one looks on her skin. She also talks more about sunscreen, and honestly, she's sold the effects of sunscreen so much, I make a mental note that that's how I should spend my next allowance. See? She's really good at this influencer stuff. Way to go, Mel!

"I think that's all the time we have for today," Mel says after she's put on some very bright pink lipstick and blotted it off. "Make sure to follow my channel, and of course, help Celia rocket to *Monster Village* stardom. She deserves it."

"And follow Gamer Girls!" I interject quickly, shoving my face into the frame.

I manage to get my words in right before Mel cuts me off by pulling me into the same hug that she did last week, though this time, also with Brooke and Jenn. And then we power down the stream. As the last light goes off, Mel immediately starts putting everything away, and makes a separate pile for me, with two smaller piles for Brooke and Jenn. I see my pile is a few extra purses and some more promotional things she received this week.

"I've never livestreamed with four people. Today was fun," Mel says.

"It was the best!" says Brooke.

"I also have a surprise for you, Celia." Mel rushes

to her desk and takes something out of her drawer.

I notice what it is immediately—it's a handheld game console. Mel has *Monster Village* pulled right up. I try to bat away the jealousy that's percolating within me. I mean, there's no way I can just buy a console like that, but I guess buying stuff comes easy for Mel (and Brooke—and Jenn).

"I wanted to see what it's all about. And you're right—this is really fun. I think we're all going to play this week. We should definitely visit each other's villages! We'll make a group chat."

I'm surprised to see that Mel has gotten really into *Monster Village*. I know she demo'd it last week on her regular computer, but buying the console? That was **mega supportive!**

Mel adds us all to a group chat and sends a cat eyes emoji, so we know to save it on our phones.

"I think Mom's friends were watching, by the way," Mel says. "Next stop, Fashion Week."

I shoot Mel a smile back. We did it! Now if only I can make it through the MegaBox contest . . .

CHAPTER SEVENTEEN

Claire drives me back home again, and when I arrive, it's not even that late. My friends are probably still gaming. I'm not sure—should I let them know I'm done? Or would that make them feel bad? I don't want to bother anyone, so I sit down at the kitchen table and pop open my laptop. Then I bring up *Monster Village*. The bag that Mel gave me rests on the chair next to me.

I immerse myself in the *Monster Village* world for a bit. Since I just have Saturday and Sunday left of the contest, I'm really in "last-minute remodeling" mode. Which means I'm finessing the final details of Mapache Gato Village, and working on making sure the Mapache Gato dumplings are as fun and aesthetic as they can be.

I don't notice my phone has buzzed until it does again in two minutes, on the second alert.

Hey, do you have a minute? The text message is from Nat.

Sure, what's up? I reply.

I'll give you a call.

When I see "Incoming Call—Nat Schwartz," I pick up the phone on the first ring. Since the Gamer Girls are still at Dylan's, Nat puts me on speaker, and I can hear Lucy and Jess mumble, although I can't decipher what they're saying.

"Is everything okay?" I ask. "Francis? Dylan?"

"They're fine, Celia," Nat snaps back. "We just need to chat with you. We saw Mel's livestream today. And Brooke's photo that she posted to ZipChat."

I feel my hands go cold. This is exactly what I was afraid of.

"Yeah, they surprised us—as you know, they live really close to Mel—"

"Celia, did you see Brooke's caption?" Jess asks.

Jess. The person who tries not to get involved in matters like this. My answer is "no"—I barely even use ZipChat! But I sign on anyway, pull up Brooke's account, and gasp. There it is, the photo of me at Mel's, with an incriminating caption running across the photo. It's more than incriminating, actually. It's downright awful. I would be mad if I were Nat, Lucy, or Jess, too.

The Gamer Girlz

The Gamer Girlz.

With a "z."

"Honestly, Celia, if you don't want to be part of our livestream, you can just say that. You don't have to go telling us a whole bunch of other stuff to hang out with Mel and her friends," Nat says. "We'd appreciate the honesty more than anything else."

"No!" I protest. "It wasn't like that—I promise!"

"Unfortunately, that's *exactly* what it feels like," Lucy cuts in. "I'm sorry, Celia. I don't like feeling replaced. It hurts."

"I promise, I can explain it all!" I say. "Can I come over to Dylan's? We can talk, and—"

"Celia, you're not welcome at Dylan's right now," Nat says sternly. "We'll talk about this later. Until then . . . tell Mel we say hi."

Then she hangs up.

I want to scream. In fact, I *do* scream. **"Gah!"**

I'm not a screamer by any means, but I'm so frustrated. This is officially the biggest fight we've ever been in, and the MegaBox contest entry is due tomorrow, and there's a ton of group chat texts from Mel and co. that I really, really want to ignore.

"**Gah!**" I scream again.

This gets Dad's attention.

"Cece!" Dad calls out as he scurries over. "Are you alright? Did something happen?"

Yes, something happened!

"I missed the Gamer Girls stream today to guest star on Mel's again, and her friends joined us. I figured it wouldn't be a big deal, but one of her friends posted a photo online and called us the Gamer Girlz with a z, so now my friends think I'm replacing them and are hurt," I explain.

"Did you get a chance to correct the story?" Dad asks very matter-of-fact.

I tell him that no, they didn't let me.

"I just miss playing with my friends," I admit. "Today was fun, but it wasn't like what I'm used to. Mel is really nice, but she's not Nat, Jess, or Lucy. And now I'm worried I've messed things up so badly, they'll never want me to be a Gamer Girl again."

"Hmm." Dad raises an eyebrow. "It's not fair they didn't give you a chance to speak your piece, but maybe they were feeling too bummed and needed to sit with it. It sounds like your friends are disappointed that you aren't with them all the time. I know they have their own things, but it's the first time they really have to share you. Maybe instead of wallow like this, you should make them feel really special. That's always an effective apology. Take account for your actions and make them feel special."

I think about his words. Even though everyone said they were cool with me missing the stream earlier, I realize that it probably wasn't as cool as they said. And then when I was streaming with basically the popular girls at school—okay, I can see how that hurt. And I was afraid of it, after all.

"I think you're right," I say finally.

My dad smiles. "You know, one of the best things about playing *Dungeons & Dragons* with my friends was that we didn't worry about being good at anything. We just had fun."

Hold up. Rewind. Dad just said he played *Dungeons & Dragons*?!

Dungeons & Dragons is pretty popular at our school—almost as popular as gaming is. There's also a lot of crossover, since a lot of people who play *D&D* *also* game. But the difference is that there's actual clubs for *D&D*, so it feels more social. Up until Gamer Girls was created, I've never heard of people getting together in person to game, it's more of a socially distant thing.

Dad sees my shocked expression and laughs. "Well, I'm afraid I don't play much anymore. I hardly have the time. But I used to, and I still pop into a session every now and then."

Huh. All this time, I thought that Mom and Dad were giving *me* the cold shoulder. I feel a little bad that Dad's put his hobbies on hold for work too.

"Did you play *D&D* with your best friends?" I ask him. I feel like I have a zillion questions. First, Abuelita plays chess, and now Dad does *D&D*!

"I did," Dad announces. "But sometimes, if I wasn't playing a character, I'd be the Dungeon Master, which means I'd be at the helm of the game, calling the shots. It's nice to switch it up, you know?"

Huh. I think I *do* know.

Dad leans back in his chair. "I'm sure they'll all understand if you tell them how you're feeling."

I wonder if my friends are talking about me right now. I think the answer must be yes. I hope Jess, at least, knows it's a misunderstanding.

"Think about it," Dad says with a small smile as he gets up. "I gotta go tidy my office. You should start your homework too."

"It's a Friday!" I protest. My dad laughs and I make a face. So, I try a new approach.

"Thanks for the advice," I say, because I mean it. It's nice when Dad talks to me like this, kind of like Abuelita. We don't get to do it often, but I like that he's making more of an effort lately even though he's so busy.

"I should text my friends now," I say.

"You could do that," replies Dad. "But maybe you need to take a step back for a minute. Is there anything relaxing you can do first?"

I think about that. The most relaxing things in the world for me are playing *Monster Village* and doodling. Right now, I think doodling might be the best way to clear my brain.

I pick up my bag and walk upstairs, heading into my room. It's only after I close the door and sit in silence for a little bit that I realize I haven't done any art in a while. I've been so busy gaming that all my free time has gone to playing *Monster Village*, and because of that, I've barely picked up my tablet.

I gather some of my sketchbooks, fancy paper, and markers and sit back down on my bed. I use the sketchpad first, doodling some designs until I feel like I've "practiced" enough to move on to the fancier paper.

I'm only **doodling**, so I'm not really paying attention to what I'm drawing or what I'm doing—I'm mostly doing what I'd do in *Monster Village*, drawing designs and animals and some town logos. But after a little bit, I start drawing my friends out of habit. I decide to put some of the skills I've been using in *Monster Village* to use and draw all of my friends as if they're a part of my town, making sure to give them all distinctive features. Then I add different things for them to hold and show off. Jess is holding a softball and a lacrosse stick; Lucy is holding a gaming controller and has a spider on her shoulder (she has a pet tarantula named Peter); and Nat is holding a dog (admittedly, one who is a *lot* smaller than Francis), and a pretend copy of *Alienlord*.

I put my friends in clothing I've designed for *Monster Village*, picking out the best designs I've made. Finally, I draw myself next to Lucy and Jess, holding a sketchbook and a paintbrush.

I stop to shake my hand out, because I've been drawing for so long, I'm kind of getting cramped. But when I stare at my work, I find myself smiling. I pick up my stylus again and title the drawing "THE GAMER GIRLS"—making sure to end it with an "s"—and prop it up on my night table next to my bed.

CHAPTER EIGHTEEN

With T-minus twenty-four hours until the MegaBox contest closes, and a whole bunch of drama on my plate, I'm in *crunch time* with Mapache Gato Village. I haven't heard back from Jess, Nat, or Lucy yet, and decide that Dad is right. I *do* need a minute to focus on myself. On Saturday, I eat, sleep, and play *Monster Village.* I barely even notice that Mom and Dad aren't working, because I'm so wrapped up in making sure the village is just right.

I don't hear from my friends all Saturday, which I expect. They made it super clear that they need some time away, and I respect that. I keep flashing back to when we found out Nat gamed and didn't tell us, and although it's a different situation, it's a rough spot. But at least I have a plan. And if it works . . . it'll be perfect!

Mel, Brooke, and Jenn text me a few times, mostly about *Monster Village* but also some more mundane things—I realize that one of the reasons Mel and her crew always look so good is because they apparently color-coordinate their outfits. So, on Monday, Mel will wear corduroy pants, and there's a color palette for fall hues. They ask me if I want to join in too, but I say no. I like having more friends than just the Gamer Girls, but I'm not interested in anything that can come across as exclusive.

Later that night, I open the link for the MegaBox Studioz contest. It's time to submit Mapache Gato Village. I've poured my heart and soul into it, making sure every garden was color-coordinated, the shops angled just right, and a whole collection of monsters teeming around the village. There are a few surprises too, so I cross my fingers and hope it all works out.

I don't expect to win. I mean, I may be the best player at my school, maybe even the best middle schooler, or maybe even the best person on a makeup channel's livestream. But there's thousands, probably even *millions*, of people entering this contest. If I'm a finalist at all, that's something to **celebrate**.

I make extra sure I attach Mapache Gato Village correctly, then close my eyes as I click "submit." When

I flutter them open, I see a "Thank you—submission entered!" screen. The deed is done.

The next morning I grab my phone, open the Gamer Girls chat, and send a text.

Can we talk? At my house today?

Lucy chimes in first. *It's raining, so no garden work. Fine by me.*

Jess next. One word. *Sure.*

Then Nat. *I think we all need to talk.*

I peek my head outside and Lucy isn't kidding. The rain is that quiet kind of rain, but it's still downpouring.

When Nat, Lucy, and Jess show up and kick off their rainboots, Mom introduces herself to Lucy. I keep forgetting Lucy is new to our group. I wonder if she ever felt uncomfortable with such a close-knit group of friends, and I make a mental note to ask her later. Then we gather around the kitchen table, and I give everyone an individual hug. I notice that each girl is stiffer than usual, but it's time to hash things out.

"I just wanted to say I'm sorry," I admit. "I was thinking about how you're all feeling, and I understand why it hurts. It seems like I blew you off to play at Mel's."

Jess raises an eyebrow. "You *did* blow us off to

play at Mel's," she reminds me.

"Okay, I did. But I didn't know Brooke and Jenn would be there, I promise. I thought that doing Mel's stream was a way to get us more followers."

"It *did* get us more followers," says Nat. "Actually, we got a ton. But look at the comments from yesterday. I took a screenshot."

"Oh no," I reply.

"I know I said that I want to be a big-time streamer, and I do, and I love that you all are helping me do that in a place I feel confident. But I care more about hanging with my friends than doing a stream, and it was hurtful that you weren't there," says Nat. "Maybe

I was even a little jealous. I mean, you are basically living my dream! You totally deserve it, by the way."

Jealous. I think back to my conversation with Abuelita. Maybe Gamer Girls and her chess group have more in common than I thought.

"I know that now," I admit. "And I'm really sorry. I've been feeling out of place lately because it hurt me that you weren't interested in *Monster Village.* So I was trying to find a way not to make everyone mad by playing on Mel's channel, but I made it all worse."

Jess smirks. "You definitely did, Cece."

But if Jess has a poker face, she doesn't keep it for long. She **BURSTS** out laughing!

"I'm sorry! I'm sorry!" she says. "I know this is serious and emotions are heavy, but sometimes we have to call each other out too."

Remember when I said Jess tells it like it is?

If Jess can be so honest with her thoughts, I suppose I can too.

"But you guys made a group chat without me. And that hurt me too," I say, in a voice quieter and softer than I'd like it to be.

"A group chat?" Nat asks. She giggles. "There's no

group chat without you."

My friends look genuinely confused. Then I see Lucy brighten. *"Oh!"* she says, like the most brilliant idea ever just came to her. "Well, we *have* sent a few messages through the *Alienlord* app." She takes her phone out and shows me a mobile *Alienlord* app. Sure enough, she's friends with Nat and Jess. I look down at my own name—Cece79—and see that it says, **"friend request not yet accepted."**

I'm glad that I said something. Otherwise, it would've really bothered me.

We're still chatting when an alarm *beeps* on my phone. The alarm signifies the time that MegaBox Studioz is streaming the finalists for the contest. I guess they have judges who assess villages super-fast or something. More than likely, it's a code, kind of like how your village gets rated every day.

"Do you mind if we tune in at least?" I ask. No one says no, and even though we're still on rocky ground, I pull up the livestream on my phone.

The same lady, TimberTina21, who announced the contest, is back today. I know things are getting better with my friends—at least, I *hope* they are. But I also have a secret. And I really hope we get to see it on the stream.

"Competitors have been hard at work building their villages, and now it's finally time to test their skills in front of the MegaBox judges," TimberTina21 says. "Our judges work lightning-fast, thanks to new MegaBox tech! We're announcing three finalists today, and then it'll come down to an online vote, with the winner announced on Friday."

Perfect time for the Gamer Girls stream, I think. *If I'm invited back.*

My phone starts flashing a bunch of purple colors, and I know it's time for the contest to **begin**.

"Alright! So the first design is Grey's Grotto, submitted by the *Monster Village* designer Greyson5," TimberTina21 says. A super-impressive map displays on screen. Whoever Greyson5 is, they put a lot of effort into making their grotto appear nice, cozy, and like a grotto in a lagoon. All the monsters wear mermaid tails that Greyson5 designed themselves.

"Cute, but I don't like it," Jess says. "If I saw this design in a promo ad, I wouldn't believe it's *Monster Village*. It looks like a totally different game."

I guess I kind of see what Jess is saying. Mermaids are great, but they aren't very *Monster Village*.

"Next up, we're taking a trip to the ultra-futuristic city of Monster Maniaville," says TimberTina21. On the screen, I see another user's—PurpleBedbug—village. This one, at least, looks *very Monster Village*. There's almost no customization done to the actual monsters themselves, but the whole town looks like it's covered in candy. It makes my mouth water. I wish I had a jawbreaker or something to chew on.

There's only one more finalist and I steady my breath. Since it's clear Jess has forgiven me already, she's the one to speak.

"The decision's been made, so there's no point being anxious now. We just need the results," Jess adds calmly.

I can hardly take it. TimberTina21 is doing a good job of keeping banter up on the livestream, but I can't hear any of it. I feel like I'm going to hurl.

I turn the volume up, and kind of like when I submitted the village in the first place, I close my eyes. I figure that the announcer's voice will be good enough, and I can flutter them open when I feel like.

"Our third finalist is a really special one. It's not

a submission by one person or entity. It's a submission by a whole group."

I open one eye.

Could it be . . . ?

"Everyone, give it up for Mapache Gato Village, submitted to us by the **Gamer Girls**!"

I nearly drop the phone. *I was the third finalist!*

"Oh my gosh, what?" Nat barks.

"Cece! No WAY!" cheers Jess.

"Holy raccoon-cats!" shouts Lucy.

But I need them to stop talking so the rest of the village can be shown.

"Shh," I reply. "Keep watching."

TimberTina21 takes users through my submission, Mapache Gato Village. And here's my secret—I took Dad's advice. I wanted to take account for my actions by apologizing and do something nice for my friends. That's why I made this a **GROUP SUBMISSION!**

The village is still in the shape of Mapache Gato, and it has neatly lined rosebushes, the perfect shops, etc., but it's also got four statues in the center of the village—one of me, Lucy, Nat, and Jess. The plaque says "Gamer Girls." It's the exact same drawing I made before but embodied forever in *Monster Village.*

What's more, I added the Gamer Girls' Den next to a shelter in one of my rosebush fields, and I named the shelter "Dylan's Animal Care" after Dylan, of course. The den has a ton of a user's favorite things, as well as unlimited junk food (it wouldn't be the Gamer Girls' Den without it) and a place for monsters to rest, kind of like how Francis and other animals rest at our own digs.

The livestream continues giving a tour of Mapache Gato Village, and all the different things I gave it. There's a basketball court called Jess's Court and a Venice Beach–inspired boardwalk named Lucy Beach. Then the tour is done.

"So, that's it, everyone. Three different choices. Voting begins shortly, so cast those votes, and we'll announce the winner on Friday. Good night, and good luck to the finalists!"

The livestream powers down.

"Oh my gosh!" Nat exclaims. "Cece, that was *incredible.* I can't believe you put that much into *Monster Village*! And you made all of us right in it."

"I did," I smile back. "I wanted to show you how sorry I am."

Now Nat looks uncomfortable.

"I think I should apologize too. I wasn't a very supportive friend to you in *Monster Village*. Not too long ago, I thought you'd never, ever game," Nat admits. "And I remember being so scared! I love that you play *Monster Village*, I really do. But I've never shared the gaming space with anyone else before. Sometimes, even battling Lucy, it feels strange. And then to see my best friend in a game I don't even know? Talk about weeeeeeeird. But I promise you, I'm going to be supportive going forward. You have my word."

"Me too," says Lucy.

"Duh," adds Jess.

"I understand now," I reply. "And I think that's a reason I liked going to Mel's. She was so interested in playing *Monster Village*. She still is. But like we said earlier, we're not a clique. We can all be gamer girls, though we're the Gamer Girls *stream*."

The four of us reach our arms out to hold one another's hands. It's a secret handshake that Nat, Jess, and I invented when we were in fifth grade, and we recently added Lucy to the mix. It basically means, **"friends forever and ever."**

No matter how popular I am now, no matter how much my friends think I'm getting all this attention for gaming, no matter how many times Liam comes up to me, no matter how many views Mel gets on her channel, my "coolness" isn't going to last. There's always going to be some new obsession or video game craze that will be the next big thing, and I definitely won't always be the "best" at it.

Maybe it'll be *Alienlord* again, and Nat and Lucy will be the ones who get all the attention. Maybe it'll be a board game. Or maybe it'll be something completely different that none of us have ever played before! Either way, I want to cheer my friends on. And now I know that I really am a gamer girl. I may not defeat aliens or score the highest points in *Alienlord*, but I'm great at cozy games, and cozy games are real and valid too.

"So . . ." I bite down on my lip. "Are we still the Gamer Girls?"

"Uh, we never *stopped* being the Gamer Girls," Lucy says with a grin. "Even if one of our members became some big-time *Monster Village* star."

"Hey!" I say with a laugh. "I'm only a *pretend* big-time *Monster Village* star. Well, until Mapache Gato

Village wins big-time at the contest. Which we'll find out on Friday."

Next week! That reminds me. I go to my dresser and grab the illustration that I made of the Gamer Girls. Since I noticed that the walls in the Gamer Girls' Den were bare, I was thinking we could put it up.

Thankfully, everyone loves the idea.

"I'll use my babysitting money next week to buy this a really cool photo frame," Lucy says. "But I'll need help picking it out."

"Done and done," says Jess. "Group-text us the images and we'll give you our opinions."

"And we'll make sure it's a group text, not in the *Alienlord* app," Nat adds with a smile. She gives me a thumbs-up. Something tells me they won't be using the app as a group text medium any more.

Somehow, the idea of picking out a photo frame sounds really fun. It's pretty basic, but I guess when you're with your BFFs, anything can be fun.

We spend the rest of the day talking about anything and everything—even a little *not* about video games, which Jess says she appreciates. I feel on top of the world. Win or lose the contest, I have my friends back, and that's all that matters.

After the Gamer Girls leave, I decide to text Mel. A lot of my *Monster Village* confidence came from her in the first place. I don't know what our future friendship looks like, but it would be nice to bring Mel into the fold, even only slightly. I just have to remember to keep showing up for my other friends too.

As I eat Dad's tacos for dinner on Sunday night, I smile to myself. The Gamer Girls are here to stay. And that's the only thing that matters.

Not even Liam Porter . . . okay, you get the gist.

Now if I can only wait until Friday!

THE END

of Book 2 in the Gamer Girls series!

Want more GAMER GIRLS fun?

Gamer Girls: Gnat vs. Spyder is available now!

Gamer Girls: Out of Control

will be available in Spring 2024

at a store or library near you.